Malicious Acts

By

Vivienne Diane Neal

Credits: Cover page: Original Sin 1 Photo: © Tmcnem | Dreamstime.com

ISBN-13: 978-0-578-07911-0
ISBN-10: 0-578-07911-9

Dedicated to my mother

I wish to thank all of my relatives, friends and customers for purchasing my books and for providing me with comments and constructive feedback.

Contents

Introduction…vi

Wicked Paradise…1

Dial D for Deception…44

Crossing Paths…68

Blind Faith…91

Serenity on Fire…120

About the Author…157

Sites to Visit…158

Introduction

Malicious Acts, a collection of five fictional short stories, is about several characters that will stop at nothing to get what they want. If it means disguising themselves as benevolent individuals and destroying lives along the way, they are up for the thrill. They will use money, romance, lust, sex, greed, deceit, and revenge as preludes to suck unsuspecting people out of their life's savings.

Paradise Baptiste wanted to have it all by any means. Through lust, sex, and manipulation, she was going to make her dreams a reality, and the man she met on an online dating site would unwittingly fulfill those dreams.

Dafoe Tang, a married man and the co-founder of a successful real estate agency, hired Tiana Bates, a naïve teen. He became her boss, mentor, and lover. The tryst lasted for six years, but when he fired her, the affair came to an abrupt end. She was determined to get even and make him pay for his lies and deception, but a message left on her answering machine would thwart those plans, and a devious plot was about to take place that would lead to her downfall.

Harry Goto thought he was the world's smartest con artist and above reproach. Soon, the tables would turn, and his cunning acts would have disastrous consequences.

Faith Bell was a fashion designer. She took over her mother's House of Fashions and had great plans for the company, but a rejection from several banks for a business loan, a call from an alluring stranger, and an unforeseen event would detour those dreams and leave her and the business in complete chaos.

Serenity Jones, a freelance illustrator, was leaving a Christmas party. Due to an unexpected blizzard, she decided to take a cab; most were off duty, and some unoccupied cabs passed her by. As she headed for the bus stop, a driver honked his horn, got her attention and stopped. When she got into his cab, her ride would become a nightmare on treachery road.

You can recover from a broken heart, but the theft of one's nest egg because of deception may never be fully recovered.

Vivienne Diane Neal

Wicked Paradise

"It is time to say good night. We have been talking for almost four hours, and I cannot wait to see you. Christmas is just around the corner. I plan to come to New York during that time and will contact you soon with my itinerary. In the meantime, stay well my darling," said the man on the other end of the phone.

"And you as well, my sugar plum," whispered the woman on the other end.

It was Labor Day, and Paradise Baptiste had just gotten off the phone with Moodie Heel, a man she met on an online dating site. For nearly six months, they e-mailed each other and eventually talked on the telephone. Based on his e-mail messages and telephone conversations, he would be the perfect pawn for a depraved act, which she was about to commit.

Always looking for ways to make fast and easy money, Paradise would read the classified ads in magazines and newspapers that promoted easy to work at home schemes: You can earn thousands of dollars every month, stuffing envelopes, processing e-mails or participating in paid surveys.

The promises of making lots of money were a big turn-on for her, but soon, the excitement would slowly dissipate. The old saying, *if it sounds too good to be true, it is probably a sham* was always the outcome.

Most of the time, she ended up spending more money than she was making and realized that these ads were nothing more than come-ons or downright rip-offs.

Marveling at how these businesses were able to advertise continuously intrigued her; she believed these companies must have been pulling in big bucks in order to keep advertising. Ad rates were certainly not cheap.

She finally recognized that these enterprises made their money by duping vulnerable and desperate people. She would send the requested payment, thinking she was going to strike it rich overnight, only to discover there were never any jobs. Instead, these companies would either send a two-page guide explaining how one could make money or provide a list of businesses that were hiring people to work from home. To continue making money, she would have to send that same guide to others, who were looking to earn extra cash and charge them anywhere from two to five dollars per lead.

There were many other get rich quick ideas, which she participated in, but it was the same old story: Paying out more money but getting zilch in return.

Since many of these structures were pyramids or multi-level-marketing tactics, she would have to keep recruiting people to make money, while the few people at the top were getting richer and richer. If she were going to become prosperous, she would have to come up with a better gig.

When Paradise was a little girl, her mother would always say, "You can marry a rich man as well as a poor man. Why settle for a man who has an empty bank account?"

For ten years, Paradise worked as a checkout clerk at a major supermarket in New York City. Her parents were now deceased, and she had no contact or relationship with other family members. She lived in a rent-stabilized studio apartment, in an old tenement building, on the Lower East Side. Most of the residents were couples with children and retirees living on social security, limited or fixed incomes. Being young, single, and childless, she had nothing in common with her neighbors and kept to herself.

She did read singles' magazines and sometimes wrote to a few of the male advertisers, but most of the men who answered her were married. She was never into sharing or wanting to be anyone's mistress.

Yet, finding a well-to-do suitor in a supermarket was never going to happen. Most of the male shoppers were penniless or unemployed. The last thing she needed in her life was someone who was living from hand to mouth. She wanted to live the good life and decided it was time to make her dreams a reality. If she did nothing else, she was going to have it all on someone else's tab.

Moodie was an actuary for a large insurance company in Detroit, Michigan. He was fifty-two years old and divorced. He and his ex-wife were married for nearly twenty years and had no children. The breakup was amicable, but six months after their divorce, she married his brother. Moodie knew the marriage was deteriorating but had no idea his wife was having an affair with his younger sibling.

The hurt and betrayal were so unbearable that he immersed himself into his work. He put in lots of overtime and worked on holidays and weekends. After accumulating a large reserve, he decided to invest that money into a start-up hedge fund. In five years, his investment grew to over two million dollars.

Paradise and Moodie shared two things: They had no offsprings, and they were both single. Other than that, they were as opposite as a spider and a worm.

He was twenty-four years her senior, well educated, sat on several corporate boards and had a six-figure income. He was average looking with a receding hairline, short in stature, and slightly overweight.

On the other hand, she was twenty-eight years old, a high school dropout and lived from paycheck to paycheck. What she lacked in refinement, she made up with her looks. She was tall, lean, and beautiful and always wore her hair closely cropped. Possessing flawless skin, she never had to wear makeup.

When it came to her sense of style, she was tacky chic. Her striking features had male shoppers flocking to her checkout counter, as if they were moths attracted to flames and asking for her phone number or a date, but she would always reject them and their advances.

Her co-workers found her to be standoffish, and unless it was work related, they rarely spoke to her.

Yet, she was the fastest checkout clerk and grocery packer in the supermarket, and as far as anyone could remember, she never came up short at the end of her shift. For three consecutive years, she was voted employee of the year.

Then rumors started to surface alleging that she was coming on to the store manager. His name was Mack Stone. Since he had a wife, Paradise made it very clear that she was not into married men. Suddenly, the gossip stopped, and six months later, he left.

The scuttlebutt was that Mack had asked Paradise to sleep with him, promising to promote her to assistant store manager if she did, but she rejected him and his proposition. To get back at her, he started to spread rumors that she was sexually harassing him. He was trying to ignore her, gave her verbal warnings to stop bothering him, but she became more aggressive, making the situation more volatile.

So eventually, he reported her to Human Resources and thought by spreading these false accusations, the company would fire her, and he would get his retribution, but the tables were about to turn on him.

While management was investigating Mack's allegations, something out of the ordinary happened. One day, an auditor came into the supermarket. While going over the books, the accountant discovered that fifty thousand dollars went into Mack's bank account and was withdrawn a week later.

It was never quite clear how the money got into his account or where it went afterwards, because he swore, "I did not steal that money, have no idea how the money got into my account or where the money went."

His options were to return the money and leave quietly, or management would press charges against him for grand larceny and embezzlement. Mack replaced the money and resigned without protest, and the company cleared Paradise of all accusations.

Ultimately, Paradise went on the Internet, where there were more options to find a man of means. She came across a dating club for millionaires, whose incomes ranged from six to seven figures. There were doctors, lawyers, bankers, CEOs of fortune 500 companies, sportspersons, entertainers, media moguls, and entrepreneurs, all searching for the ideal mate.

Over twenty five hundred marriages had taken place from connections made through their service since its launch five years ago, and the site was getting over two million hits a month. For the next several weeks, she was reading various profiles, when one particular ad caught her attention:

Single and lonely man, in his early fifties, desires to meet a nice young woman for a relationship leading to marriage. My income is over five hundred thousand dollars a year. I am romantic, considerate, kind, and generous. Traveling, reading poetry, and stamp collecting are some of my favorite activities. Your looks, status, and income are unimportant. Truthfulness is a very important characteristic that I look for in a woman. If you wish to know more, drop me an e-mail along with your photo.

When Paradise read that ad, she quickly sent an e-mail along with her photo and waited for his reply. Five days later, she heard from him. To say her beauty struck him was accurate. When he saw her picture, he wrote, *I know love when I see it*.

For the next several months, they e-mailed each other. He wrote how his ex-wife and brother had betrayed him, and pain like that never disappears until you find that special someone. When they started conversing by phone, Moodie knew then that Paradise was going to be his wife.

On Thanksgiving Day, Moodie called Paradise with his travel plans. He would arrive in New York on December 22 and return home after the New Year.

Since her apartment was too tiny to accommodate two people, she recommended a hotel that was within walking distance to her building.

They talked for almost three hours and made plans to attend a couple of holiday festivities. He could not wait to see her.

In his brain, he had it all planned and thought, *I will ask Paradise to marry me on Christmas day, take her back to Detroit, retire and travel the world with my beautiful young bride. It will be a romantic fairytale followed by eternal happiness.*

Meanwhile, Paradise had put in for vacation. She had two weeks coming but only requested one week; she was planning to return to work on January 2 if her plot failed. Just like Moodie, she had elaborate plans.

She fixed up the apartment, bought some cheap sexy lingerie, went to an African herbalist and purchased some aphrodisiacs, extracts, aromatic herbs and spices, all with hypnotic powers. These ingredients were so potent that if consumed in large amounts would leave an individual in a zombie state for days.

All the trappings were now in place, and she was preparing to meet him head-on. Like a scorpion, she was ready to inflict pain on an unsuspecting target.

At 2 PM, Moodie's plane arrived at JFK International Airport. He got a cab, went straight to the hotel and called Paradise. So delighted to hear his voice, she invited him over for dinner that evening and gave him walking directions to her place.

He could not wait to see her and quickly unpacked, took a shower and grabbed a snooze for a couple of hours. He wanted to be bright eyed and bushy tailed for his soon-to-be lifetime partner.

The doorbell rang, and Paradise was ready to play the most malicious role of her life. When she opened the door, there stood Moodie, looking like a lost prince, waiting for his beautiful princess to show him the way and smiling as if he were a flea stuck in a dog's mane. She had the biggest beam on her face, and the two hugged and kissed for almost three minutes. He was so stimulated that he gradually fell to the floor, and she landed on top of him.

They started to undress each other and made love like two felines in heat. In their sexually charged state, they screamed and moaned as though the world was about to end. The lovemaking went on all night, until they finally fell asleep.

When Paradise and Moodie woke up, it was almost ten o'clock in the morning. He kissed her and then whispered, "Good morning, my little honey bun; when we made love last night, I finally found true love; will you accept my hand in marriage?"

Holding his hand firmly and in a low-keyed voice, she said, "And good morning to you, sweet pea; it would be an honor to be your wife."

They dressed, had breakfast and arranged to have dinner at her place on Christmas Day.

"Can I bring anything?" he asked.

"No, just bring you. Dinner will be served at 6 PM."

He left feeling like a teenager who just got lucky with the new girl on the block, jogged back to his hotel and called a business associate who was a diamond broker. He placed a rush order for an engagement ring, which would arrive at his hotel by special courier on Christmas Eve.

On Christmas Day, Paradise had prepared an elaborate feast, fit for an emperor and a drink that would leave Moodie in an erotic stupor. She wore a red see-through thong, a black laced camisole, and green stilettos and sprayed her body with gardenia perfume.

At exactly 5:45 PM, the doorbell rang. When she opened the door, Moodie was standing there with his eyes and mouth wide opened and carrying a small colorful shopping bag. When he entered her place, she removed his coat and escorted him to the dinner table. Being so elated, he excused himself and dashed into the bathroom. He stayed in there for five minutes. After getting his faculties together, he walked into the dining area.

The two sat down, said grace and started to eat. After dinner, they exchanged gifts. She gave him a pair of gold plated cuff links, a matching tie clip, and a silver-plated money clip. Yet, the biggest moment came when he gave her that shopping bag, and in that bag was a four-carat pear-shaped diamond ring. She stared at that rock, expressed gratitude and served him her exotic cocktail.

He quickly gulped it down and asked for more. Thirty minutes later, he removed her top and thong, and they went at it like two oversexed lizards in the sweltering desert. He could not get enough of her sexual escapades and kept begging her for more. She fulfilled his wishes, until he fell asleep.

The next day, Moodie was on planet desire and did not know if he were coming or going. He was completely under Paradise's domination.

She played him like an organ and asked, "Sweetie pie, how much did you pay for my ring?"

He merrily answered, "Fifty thousand dollars, my little tart."

Like a Venus flytrap, her mouth opened wide, as though she were ready to devour him. Stunned and happy, she asked for his security codes to his brokerage account. Without any hesitation, and with a big smile on his face, he gave her that information.

Later that day, Paradise walked Moodie back to his hotel. He was still in a horny frame of mind.

"I want to make more passionate love to you," he pleaded.

She said, "Hold that thought. I have a big surprise for you and will return in a couple of hours."

He insisted, "Please, hurry back. I don't know how long I can keep it up."

She kissed him on the lips, left his room and went straight to an Internet café. She logged on to his account and moved all of his money into an offshore account. On December 27, she packed her bags and left New York.

When Moodie came around in his hotel room, it was January 2. He was in a mystified and an aroused state but had no recollection as to what took place during the past several days. All he could remember was checking into the hotel and going to meet a woman, whose name he could not remember.

He went through his luggage and found a receipt for a diamond ring but had no idea as to why he bought the ring or for whom. On the slip was the contact information; he called to inquire about the purchase.

The jeweler said, "You ordered the ring for your fiancée."

If Moodie was confused then, he was about to get news that would leave him in a state of rage. According to his airline ticket, he would return to Detroit on January 3.

After arriving home, Moodie was fatigued and went straight to bed. Because his head was in such disarray, he had difficulty falling asleep. He decided to get up and go online.

"You got mail," said the voice, which somewhat startled him. He opened the post, and in it was the following message:

Verification for the transaction executed on December 26 is now available. You will need your user name and password to view this confirmation. We wish to thank you for trusting your account with our brokerage firm.

Since he could not remember his user name and password, he sent an e-mail requesting them. When he received the information and logged on to his account, his money was gone.

Seconds later, he felt a sharp pain in his head and started to have flashbacks as to what took place in New York. After getting his memory back, he realized that an evil tarantula had conned him out of 2.5 million dollars. He sat there and started to scream and wail, but his tears quickly turned to anger. He immediately contacted law enforcement in New York City and filed a complaint.

To question her, the police went to Paradise's apartment, but she was long gone. When the officers questioned the neighbors, no one could tell the detectives very much, because she never spoke to or socialized with any of the residents. The same was true at the workplace. She came to work, did her job and went home. Being a loner and a secretive person, she would have made a great covert operative. Like a silhouette, Paradise was a complete blur.

In no time, the scandal traveled throughout the community about Paradise duping a man out of his millions. Many saw her as someone who lacked the aptitude to carry out such a deception. Most of the neighbors could not comprehend how she was able to con any man out of his money.

The employees at the supermarket could not believe that such a seemingly quiet and conscientious worker would have the inclination to commit such an illicit act. Then the staff started to guess that she was probably responsible for taking that fifty thousand dollars from the company, placing it into the store manager's account and then removing it to God knows where.

What folks did not know was that Paradise could be a merciless person if crossed. When Mack started those vicious tales about her coming on to him, he did not realize it then, but he made the biggest faux pas of his existence.

A year went by, and Moodie had not heard from the police regarding the whereabouts of Paradise and his money. He knew it was pointless to continue hounding them. By now, the case was cold. *If Paradise was smart enough to get all of my money, she would not have been so foolish to leave a paper trail*, he concluded.

Retiring from his job was now out of the question, and as far as looking for love, he decided that being alone was a much better alternative.

Paradise was now living on the island of Madagascar. Before her arrival, she had cosmetic surgery on her face. The surgeon did a superb job, because she was now more beautiful than words could explain. She would have been unrecognizable if Moodie saw her, and he probably would have fallen for her without any hesitation.

She was still attracting men, like hungry pit bulls going after fresh meat, but she would continue to ignore them. Thanks to Moodie, the cash she stole from him was all she needed; his money would take care of her for a very long time.

After living in Madagascar for nearly five years, Paradise's dreams of having it all had finally come true. She lived on an estate, ten minutes from the town of Diego-Suarez, which was right off the beach. The colonial style home sat on three acres of land with a beautiful view overlooking the French Bay. The structure of the property was of distinctive quality and had an actual stairway manually assembled into a rock that led up to the garden level, where she resided.

The property came with six bedrooms, six marble bathrooms, a living room and dining area, a sitting room, an adjoining chef's kitchen, and an office. All of the rooms had French windows, roller shutters, mosquito screens, and a view of the ocean.

Heating was not normally needed, but there was a solar paneling installed by the previous owner. The hot water was electric, and the house's double ceilings provided great insulation. The window frames were rosewood. There was a septic tank for drainage. A fountain, which increased the permanent supply of water, irrigated the beautiful garden.

On the lower grounds, was a guesthouse, which came with three-bedrooms, three full bathrooms, a spacious kitchen, an extended dining room for entertaining, and an enclosed patio. A two-story commercial loft and the caretaker's residence were behind the guesthouse.

She paid six hundred and fifty thousand dollars for the estate, but the best deal was the sixty dollars per year property tax.

To bring in additional income, Paradise rented out the guesthouse to vacationers, who would enjoy complete solitude and the amenities of being close to the airport, high-end shops, nightclubs, and restaurants. Guests also had access to a private beach, golf course, and tennis court.

She charged six hundred dollars per room/per day with a minimum stay of three days. If a family or group wanted to rent the entire guesthouse for one month, the cost was fifty thousand dollars.

To attract tourists, she ran ads in travel publications and on the Internet. To avoid interacting with the guests, she hired a concierge service to handle all reservations, housekeeping, landscaping, menu and meal planning, and grievances. The top level of the house was off limits to guests, but they had free range of the lower grounds. In no time, her venture became a success.

In its third year, the business made over one million dollars in profits. By the island's standard of living, she was a wealthy woman; yet, the old adage, *what goes around comes around*, was always in the back of her mind.

Being a charlatan, she knew there was the likelihood that someone would be lurking in the bushes and trying to con her out of her stolen wealth but would always recap, *I met a rich man once, took all of his money and will have no problems doing it again.*

Spending money was Paradise's greatest pastime. She wore high-fashion couture, had enough ornaments to open a jewelry store and a huge collection of shoes, which would have made Imelda Marcos green with envy. Paradise was living high on the hog.

Because of her flamboyant lifestyle, people were forever inviting her to various social functions, but despite all of her money and the power that came with it, she was still cautious when it came to strangers.

Even though she had her face completely altered, there was forever the possibility that someone would recognize her.

She often thought about Moodie, wondered if he still lived in Detroit and went back to the first day they met. She often asked herself, *What on earth did this his ex-wife actually see in him? He would have never made the front cover, center page, or back cover of any men's fashion magazine. On a scale of one to ten, he was a two, but his money compensated for all of his shortcomings.*

Christmas was approaching, and Paradise was becoming somewhat restless. She came up with an idea and called directory assistance to see if Moodie was still living in Detroit. To her astonishment, he was. From a distance, she was eager to see him and scrutinize his movements. She was confident that he would never recognize her and wanted to see if she could seduce him again, but after careful consideration, she scratched that idea. He was probably still broke, and she no longer needed cash. Even though she was frivolously spending money, her business was bringing in lots of dough to replenish her high expenditures.

Her total assets were now worth over three million dollars, which she kept in an offshore account in Panama and under the corporation, Beach Island Inn. If she ever had to leave Madagascar because of some political, economic, or social upheaval, her reserves would be safe and easy to acquire.

Every week, Paradise would receive a schedule of visitors who made reservations to stay in her guesthouse. While going over the roster, she almost fell off the chair and could not believe whose name was on that register.

Moodie Heel was going to be spending a week in the guesthouse.

She sat there for almost an hour, and in a panic state thought, *What a fluke that Moodie is coming to Madagascar. Is he on to me, and if so, should I pack and leave?*

After calming down, she became conscious that he had no idea where she was, and if he did, would have no jurisdiction to have her arrested. Besides, he would never recognize her. Still, she did not want to take any chances and decided to leave for Panama until he left Madagascar.

She wanted to play it safe and left the following instructions to the concierge service: "I am leaving for vacation, and my name should never come up if anyone inquires about me."

The service understood and would answer all inquires by saying, "Due to our privacy rules, we are not at liberty to release the names of our guests, renters, or owners of the estate. If you wish, you may leave your contact information, and someone will get back to you shortly."

She provided the service with an extra bonus for keeping her secret, left a week before Moodie was to arrive and would return after he left.

On Friday afternoon, Moodie arrived in Madagascar. When he got to the guesthouse, a feeling of déjà vu came over him. Since this was his first time visiting the island, he was puzzled as to why he felt this way.

Going on the advice of a business associate, he came to check on the various products for his small spice shop back in Detroit. Coffee, vanilla, and cloves were some of Madagascar's most popular commodities. The next day, he was going to meet with a food broker.

In the meantime, he unpacked his bags and took a warm bath. As he sat in the tub, his mind started to wonder back to Paradise. He believed she did him a huge favor by swindling him out of his money, because he would have never known that his true vocation was to be an entrepreneur.

When his money disappeared, he had nothing but his house, which he received in the divorce settlement; he only had to worry about property tax, utilities, insurance, and up-keep costs. However, six months later, he received a layoff notice along with a nice severance package. Although he had thirty years experience in the actuary business, finding work at his age was not an easy task, and prospective employers were offering entry-level salaries. In most cases, he was overqualified.

In addition, the country was going through an economic meltdown, and many companies were laying off workers, cutting back or not hiring at all. With no luck in finding a job in his field, he thought about going back to school and pursuing another career, but fate changed all of that, and an unexpected opportunity came his way.

After attempting to find work for almost a year, Moodie decided to visit a local college. He was not quite sure what he wanted to do or what classes to take. While he was reading the materials, his cell phone rang.

"Hello, Moodie Heel speaking."

"Hi Moodie, this is Thomas Reed; how are you?"

Moodie responded, "I am doing fine; thank you for asking. I was just looking through some brochures and thinking about going back to school. At my age, it has not been easy finding a job."

Thomas said, "I understand what you are going through; things are really bad, and this is why I called you. I have a client who is looking to sell his spice shop because of a sudden illness in his family, and I thought about you. You are great with people and have excellent managerial skills, and I believe this would be a great opportunity for you. Many people who are having difficulties finding work usually try their hands at starting their own business. The quaint little shop is located in the Renaissance Center, is debt-free and has a large inventory and loyal customers. The lease will expire in three years. The store has been in existence for seven years. Since the owner is willing to negotiate a fair selling price, perhaps you'd be interested in meeting with him."

Without giving it another thought, Moodie replied, "Yes, I would like to meet with the owner."

Thomas was an attorney who specialized in business and commercial real estate law. Moodie had known him for over thirty years and had complete faith in him to act on his behalf. Moodie refinanced his home and bought the shop for five hundred thousand dollars.

For the first year, a consultant worked with him until he was confident enough to run the business on his own. Two years later, the spice shop made close to two million dollars in sales. He repaid the loan against his home, and the Renaissance Center offered him a ten-year lease. His shop now had an assistant manager, two full-time and two part-time employees.

After mesmerizing about Paradise, Moodie got out of the tub and got dressed. In his room was a directory of restaurants, shops, nightspots, and sightseeing tours. He decided to eat at a seafood restaurant, which was not too far from the guesthouse. While eating, he still could not get Paradise out of his head. *Why does she keep reoccurring in my psyche?* he wondered.

After finishing his meal, he walked back to the guesthouse but was distracted by the house on the upper level and thought, *Wow, what a beautiful place. I wonder if anyone is staying or living there.*

With his digital camera, he took several pictures of the structural design. After returning to his room, he began looking at the images. All of a sudden, sensual feelings started to explode inside of him.

Why are these emotions occurring now? He could not make the connection between the photos of the house and his emotions. The last time he felt this way, he was with Paradise. He then laughed and concluded that because he was thinking about her, his mind was playing tricks on him. He put the camera away and turned in for the night.

The next morning, Moodie went into town to meet with the food rep. After sampling some of the island's premium coffee, vanilla, sugar, and spices, he placed an order. The merchandise would reach his shop in several days by air.

On his way back to the guesthouse, he ran into the ground's keeper and asked, "Is the house at the top a bread and breakfast and if so, is anyone staying there?"

The worker answered, "That house is privately owned and occupied; guests are not allowed on that level."

Moodie said, "Thank you, and have a nice day."

The caretaker replied, "Thank you sir. If I can be of additional assistance, please let me know."

Watching that house became Moodie's obsession. In two days, he was planning to return to Detroit, but because the house had such a riveting effect on him, he decided to stay an extra week. He could not explain his odd or compulsive behavior.

Since he reserved his room for only one week, and a group of vacationers had booked his and the other two rooms for the next two weeks, he had to leave. He made reservations at another inn.

He called the shop and informed his assistant manager that he would be staying an extra week, and she should be on the lookout for a shipment of goods.

On Saturday morning, Moodie checked into a cottage, which was a ten-minute walk to the enticing house. He wanted to know who owned the estate and called the concierge service, but to obtain that information was like extracting teeth from a crocodile.

Whatever questions he asked, the responses were always the same: "That information is strictly confidential."

He decided to take matters into his own hands. First thing Monday morning, he would visit the occupant and act as an interested homebuyer.

When Moodie woke up Monday morning, it was a cloudy day. He skipped breakfast and headed for the intriguing house. When he walked up the stairs and rang the doorbell, there was no answer. While looking around, he thought he saw the vague likeness of a woman coming towards him, but she quickly disappeared. At first, he thought he was hallucinating but blamed his confusing state for not eating. He decided to go back to the inn, have breakfast and would return on Tuesday.

Paradise had returned home late Monday evening and was certain that Moodie was gone. Drained from the long plane ride, she decided to turn in for the night. The next day, she woke up feeling free from anxiety. Moodie was gone, and it would be back to business as usual.

She saw the empty refrigerator and decided to go to the market. As she was getting ready to leave, a feeling of alarm came over her.

In a panic state, she voiced, *Why on earth is he still here? I thought that idiot left last Friday.* She quickly called the concierge service and learned that Moodie did check out on Friday. *But why is he still here and on his way up those stairs?* she pondered.

Suddenly, the doorbell rang. In her cool, calm, and collected manner, she opened the door.

With a phony smile on her face, she said, "Good morning, may I help you?"

"And good morning to you, my name is Moodie Heel. I hope I did not disturb you. For some reason, I was lured to this house. Are you the owner of this elegant estate?"

For a split second, she did not know how to answer him and asked, "May I inquire what your interest is in this property?"

He replied, "I wish I had the answers, but I do not. This place is so beautiful; it called out to me."

"Well, I had those same feelings and signed a two year lease, which will be up soon," she said.

He then asked, "Does the owner of this house live in Madagascar?"

She replied, "I do not know, because I rented this house from the concierge service."

"Oh yes, I asked them about this place, but they would not release that information to me."

She then said, "Perhaps you'd be interested in buying this house. Let me give you a tour of the place. By the way, my name is Adise."

"It is a pleasure to meet you, Adise. What a beautiful name. Does it have a significant meaning?"

"No, it is a combination of my parents' first names, which were Adam and Denise," was her answer.

Adise showed Moodie the house. Immensely attracted to her, he sensed there was a connection between them, as though they might have met in a previous life. He was beginning to fall for her, but he swiftly came back to his senses. His mind drifted back to that horrible episode with Paradise. He decided to keep his distance with Adise. Yet, she was tempting, and once again, he would fall under her magic charm.

After looking at the property and taking notes, Moodie wanted to buy the estate. He was willing to pay top dollars and understood why the place had such a command over him. The house was meant to be his.

Adise encouraged him to pursue the matter and invited him to have dinner with her on Thursday. With great enchantment, he accepted her enticement and would contact the concierge service first thing in the morning.

After he left, she quickly called the service and said, "Someone will be contacting you about buying my estate. I wish to meet with you at once."

Fifteen minutes later, the manager arrived at her home.

"Thank you for coming on such short notice. A Mr. Moodie Heel is interested in buying my property. He will be calling you tomorrow, but he must never know that I am the owner. The corporation, Beach Island Inn, will handle all of the details. My asking price is two million dollars. I am certain he will accept this offer, and if he does, your service will receive a nice commission."

The executive with a humongous smile on his face said, "All matters will be handled in the utmost and strictest confidence. Please know that your identity will never be revealed." She thanked him and got down to business.

On Wednesday morning, Moodie called the concierge service.

"Hello, this is Moodie Heel. I stayed at your guesthouse last week. Recently, I had an opportunity to see the entire estate. If the owner is willing to sell, I would like to buy the property."

The manager said, "I will have to contact the proprietors and see if they are interested in selling. If you give me your contact information, I'll get back to you at the end of the week."

Moodie was planning to fly back to Detroit on Friday afternoon and did not know when he would be returning to Madagascar. The manager assured him that all exchanges could take place by e-mail if Moodie did not hear from the service by Friday morning.

While sitting in his room, Moodie was anxious; he was hoping the association would agree to sell him the estate. Later that afternoon, his phone rang. It was the manager.

"Hello, Mr. Heel, I contacted the owners, and they are eager to sell you the property. Their asking price is two million dollars."

Moodie thought long and hard, but for what he was getting, the price was a steal. Back in Detroit, the asking price for property like that would be over twenty million dollars.

"I will accept their offer and pay cash."

The manager then said, "I will contact the group, inform them of your intent to buy and send all the necessary papers to the address you provided on your reservation form if that is okay."

With unwavering joy, he said, "That's fine. You can send all the particulars to my home or e-mail address."

Later that evening, Paradise received the news that Moodie was going to buy the property; she was now ready to make her final move.

It was Thursday evening. Paradise called the concierge service and ordered Grilled Salmon with Basil and Mint Sauce, Wild Rice, Julienne Carrots, Chocolate Mousse, and Korus Cabernet. Even though she was an excellent cook, she wanted to avoid any stimulants that would make Moodie suspicious; she would play the role of a woman who could not boil water, even if her life depended on it.

At exactly 7:30, the doorbell rang; happy as a bee that was about to sting a gullible mark, she opened the door. It was Moodie looking sharp in his three-piece purple suit and red shoes; he handed her a pink carnation. She invited him in and thanked him for the flower.

In a lifting voice, he said, "The owners agreed to sell me this estate, and their asking price was too good to pass up."

She sat there with a smirk on her face and said, "Congratulations! I know you will love living here. The people on this island are very friendly and helpful. I will certainly miss this place."

He asked, "Do you live in this house alone? It is an enormous place for one person."

"Yes, I live here alone, but my relatives and friends visit Madagascar often and stay here as my guests."

The two started to eat, with Moodie doing most of the talking. All of a sudden, he blurted, "You are the most beautiful woman I have ever seen; have you ever done any modeling?"

All she could do was not burst out laughing and said, "No, but I do enjoy reading fashion magazines."

Suddenly, the two started to express amusement.

After dinner, they continued to chat. While sipping his wine, Moodie started to become sexually aroused. Adise sensed that he was ready for her and got closer to him. They started to tongue kiss, slowly undressed each other, ended up on the floor and made love like two individuals who had no physical contact for eons.

Their naked bodies were moving up and down like two erotically charged grasshoppers, but in his heated and blissful state, he screamed, "Paradise! Paradise! Please, do not stop! Oh Paradise! Oh Paradise! Rock me baby!"

All of a sudden, the lovemaking came to a screeching halt.

For a split-second, she thought, *Oh no, he knows who I am.*

Embarrassed, he said, "Adise, forgive me. I don't know what came over me."

In a pseudo indignant tone, she asked, "Who on earth is Paradise. Is she your wife?"

"No, I am divorced. Paradise was someone I met a long time ago and do not want to bore you with all the ghastly details."

He quickly got dressed, apologized again for his outburst, thanked her for the lovely dinner and scurried out of that house, as if he were a frightened mouse being chased by a seething cat.

It was close to midnight when Moodie arrived in Detroit. The next day, he went to the shop. The shipment had arrived. Until the title to the estate was in his possession, he would wait before telling his staff the good news.

He had big plans for the property. He would turn the guesthouse into a time-share, convert the upper level of the house into a bed and breakfast and use the same concierge service to manage the establishment.

Two months later, Moodie received the documents that would transfer title of the estate to him. He had Thomas read over the papers, and everything was in order.

Moodie wired two million dollars into Beach Island Inn's account and was now the proud owner of one of the most elaborate estates on the island of Madagascar.

When Paradise received confirmation that the two million dollars was in her account, she jumped for joy and laughed, hysterically. She could not get over that night when Moodie called her Paradise. *He made a complete ass out of himself. It was one of my most memorable roles, and I did not have to go to Detroit. Instead, the dummy dumb, unwittingly, came to me. Now, that is E.S.P.*

Two weeks later, she left Madagascar, flew to Panama and dissolved her corporation. She had nearly five million dollars wired to her new offshore account. On the plane ride to her new destination, she reflected, *Poor old Moodie, he did not have a clue that he was being played by me again and buying the same estate twice. Life sure is grand.*

Six months later, Moodie was back in Madagascar and remodeling the house. He replaced the old fittings with elegant furnishings and created an elaborate gourmet kitchen with state-of-the art appliances. The dining area and living room became a center for entertaining. Beach Island Inn was now Ocean View Bed and Breakfast, and its grand opening would take place at the end of the year.

As Moodie was looking through his mail, there was a letter from the Royal Bank of Panama addressed to Ms.

Paradise Baptiste, Owner of Beach Island Inn. He opened the envelope, removed the letter and started to read:

Dear Ms. Baptiste:

We were sorry to hear that you closed your Beach Island Inn's corporate account. We want to thank you wholeheartedly for trusting us with your funds.

As a valued businessperson and customer, you will always be part of our banking family.

If we can ever be of further assistance to you, please do not hesitate to contact us.

Very truly yours,

Henry W. Jones, General Manager
Royal Bank of Panama

After reading that correspondence, Moodie was baffled. He started to wonder, *Is this the same Paradise Baptiste who duped me out of my money several years ago?* After examining the letter further, he recognized that Adise was the last five letters of her first name, and she must have had cosmetic surgery on her face. It was now clear that she was the anonymous proprietor of the estate. Suddenly, the blood left his face, and the room started to spin. Two minutes later, he fainted.

When Moodie regained consciousness, he understood why those strange and wonderful feelings toward the house and Adise had captivated him. *I cannot believe that scheming witch tricked me again. What is wrong with me? How could this have happened again?*

Sitting in his office and in total disbelief, Moodie started to look back on the ill-fated events that besieged his life. He questioned, *What made me a casualty of treachery three times and twice by the same woman? My ex-wife and brother committed the ultimate betrayal, and Paradise went beyond fraud and deception and played me as though I was a used fiddle.*

He always saw himself as a perceptive person when it came to business. However, when it came to his love life, he was a complete nincompoop. Until he was able to figure out what was going on inside of him, he would put off looking for love, indefinitely.

The grand opening of Ocean View Bed and Breakfast took place on New Year's Eve and was booked to full capacity. As Moodie was welcoming and wishing his guests a Happy, Healthy, and Prosperous New Year, one of the guests had a familiarity about her.

Tall, elegant, and stunning, she wore a long maroon beaded dress with a slit in the front and zebra tinted heels. When she started to walk towards Moodie, he had those same sensual feelings as he did with Paradise.

As the two were looking intensely at each other, he extended his hand to shake hers and said, "Hello, my name is Moodie Heel, and I am the owner of this inn. Welcome to Madagascar! I do hope you enjoy your stay here."

In a sexy accent, she said, "It is a pleasure to meet you, Mr. Heel, and my name is Destiny Love.■

Dial D for Deception

Tiana Bates had just gotten off the phone with a prospective client, who was interested in purchasing a new home. She was the person to go to if you were looking for an opulent address. Her fortunes came from selling million dollar mansions in the most exclusive areas of southeastern New York, which was the place to be if you had the capital and the proper lineage.

Homes were valued from three to twenty million dollars, and most of the residents were CEOs of major corporations, professionals, business owners, foreign dignitaries, celebrities, athletes, retirees, and trust fund offsprings.

Many of these people spent most of their time networking, traveling, entertaining, attending social events and volunteering at their favorite charities.

Yet, behind the pretense were individuals living from paycheck to credit cards just to maintain their lavish existence.

Growing up in a working family community, Tiana's vision was to become filthy rich and a member of the elite inner circle. She was the oldest of three girls.

Her parents owned a cleaning service whose clients included apartment complexes, condominiums, co-ops, offices, strip malls, and estates. Every weekend, she would accompany her parents to help clean these establishments.

When it came to the mansions, she was always in awe of their beauty and splendor and vowed, one day, to own a home just like the ones her parents spent so much time maintaining.

Even though Tiana's parents had a large clientele base, the family was by no means rich.

Her parents were born in St. Lucia, came to the United States in the early 1980s and worked and saved enough money to purchase a cleaning business, but with the company came outstanding debts and more headaches than an aspirin could cure.

One year later, Tiana was born, and before long, the family grew to five.

For fifteen years, her parents worked 24/7 just to break even. The money they made went right back into the business, with very little capital left for building wealth.

Because of bad management and excessive debts, the company folded. Her parents decided to sell their home and return with their two younger daughters to St. Lucia.

Since Tiana was in her last year of high school, she stayed in New York and remained in the house until it was sold.

While growing up, Tiana would overhear her parents talk about how their customers became prosperous. Most were born into wealth. Some made their money by creating their own companies, while others made their millions selling land, residential, and commercial properties.

What better way to become affluent than to work in real estate, she thought and was determined to be part of that fortunate group.

She never wanted to be in the same situation as her parents, struggling to make ends meet and ending up in debt. If it meant clawing her way to the top and using others to get there, she was ready for the challenge.

After graduating from high school, Tiana found a job as a part-time receptionist at a real estate agency. When she walked into that office to apply for the job, her beauty, charm, and innocence wooed the owner, whose name was Dafoe Tang.

After one year on the job, she became a full-time employee. He became her mentor and taught her everything about the real estate business. She got her first taste of house selling when his agency sold her parents' home. She was convinced then that working in real estate was going to be her ticket to fame and prosperity.

Soon, she and Dafoe were secretly having romantic trysts. She had just turned nineteen; he was thirty-four and married.

Five years later, she took forty-five hours of real estate courses, which Dafoe paid for, and after completing the requirements, she passed the exam on the first try and obtained her real estate salesperson's license.

At age twenty-five, Tiana was selling more upscale office buildings, condominiums, and mansions than any of her colleagues. She had an exceptional gift for getting clients, especially male buyers, to bid on estates, often sight unseen.

Many of her co-workers started to wonder if she were doing more than just showing properties to her male customers. Envy and suspicion were starting to boil over in the office. Rumors were circulating that there was more going on between Tiana and Dafoe, because she was getting top listings and exclusive areas to work.

The atmosphere around the workplace was getting so edgy that some agents threatened to leave.

Then, word got back to Hope, Dafoe's wife, about the late meetings that were taking place throughout southeastern New York. Since Hope was a silent partner and came from an influential family who provided the startup capital when the couple started the real estate business, it did not take a mentalist to figure out what the next move would be.

Hope ordered Dafoe to fire Tiana, and the six-year love affair was over.

Becoming a real estate broker was Tiana's next goal. She completed ninety hours of approved courses, passed the exam and got her real estate broker's license.

Two years later, she opened her own real estate agency on the same block where Dafoe and Hope lived.

To say *Hell hath no fury like a woman scorned* could not have been more truthful, because she was going to get her revenge by driving the couple out of the neighborhood, destroying their business and making southeastern New York her exclusive domain.

She did not hire or work with other agents, approached potential sellers to list their properties exclusively with her, bought foreclosures for next to nothing, placed them on the market and made colossal profits. She was a piranha that would crush any agent who got in her way.

By age twenty-eight, Tiana's net worth was five million dollars. Now affluent, she had no problems making it known. She lived in a split-level, 5,000 square feet house in Sag Harbor.

The home came with four bedrooms and four baths, two and a half baths, a large formal dining room, a state-of-the art kitchen, and a four-car garage. The property sat on 2.91 acres of land and came with a private beach, and a chalet with an enclosed terrace. The house cost three million dollars.

She then joined a very exclusive country club. The membership fee was fifty thousand dollars a year.

There were times when she would deliberately flaunt her wealth in front of Dafoe and Hope. Wherever the couple went, she was always there, upstaging and ingratiating herself with the couple's close friends and important business associates.

She would wear sexy and revealing outfits to magnetize Dafoe and to make Hope jealous. It was hard for him to keep his wandering eyeballs off her; he was like a dog in heat whenever he saw her.

People would observe the upset and humiliation in Hope's demeanor. Most of the country club crowd thought very little of Tiana, because she was an outsider who was dying to be one of them, and the fact that she slept with a married man, while working her way to the top, did not sit well with most of the members.

Concealment was more important than decorum. After all, half the town was doing one person or another, but the idea was to hide one's indiscretions and not broadcast them to the world.

Tiana may have lacked class, but soon, she would be the only subject matter for salacious gossip.

When Dafoe hired Tiana, she was very impressionable. He made so many promises to her that she actually believed all the rubbish that came out of his mouth, like telling her he was planning to leave his wife when he got his affairs in order.

The couple would meet in empty for-sale homes and off the beaten path motels and make zealous love for hours.

He would always utter, "You are my soul mate. My wife does not understand me the way you do, and you bring such joy into my life when we are together. I can be myself around you. At times, Hope can be frigid and never wants to try new lovemaking techniques or positions."

And Tiana would always fall for his lines. When they were together, she was always on planet desire. Sometimes the sex was so intense that she would cry out for more, so much so that her screams of joy would reverberate throughout the place.

As far as she knew, it was just a matter of time before he would divorce his wife, and Tiana and Dafoe would be working together and expanding her agency into a well-respected enterprise.

Then reality smacked her in the face, and when he fired her and turned his back on her, she finally recognized that he was never planning to leave his wife but was just using Tiana to satisfy his own carnal needs. What he could not get from Hope, he got from Tiana.

Even though she was a successful entrepreneur, she was still lonely and agonizing for passion and romance. Dafoe was her first love, and he would be a hard act to replace, but no matter how long it took, she was going to make him pay for his deception.

It was now time for Tiana to take a vacation; she decided to visit her family in St. Lucia. While there, all she thought about was Dafoe and would have visions of him and Hope going at it, as though they were two alligators in heat.

I should be the one with Dafoe, she thought and could not understand what he actually saw in his wife.

She was no raving beauty and lacked sensuality; she had cauliflower ears, bulging eyes, and humongous feet.

On the other hand, Tiana was tall, beautiful, intelligent, and ambitious, the kind of qualities she thought Dafoe admired in a woman.

Of course, money talks, and no money talks, and the fact that Hope came from old money, and he did not, would have made her look first rate in any man's eyes.

When Tiana arrived home from her trip, there were many messages on her answering machine. Most of the calls were from likely homebuyers and investors, but one message got her immediate attention:

"Hello, Mademoiselle Bates. This is Harry Goto calling. An associate gave me your name. I live in Tunisia and own a hotel. In a couple of weeks, I will be in New York. Because I plan to travel more often between my country and New York, my desire is to buy a home to use as an office and a meeting place. At your convenience, please call me. You can reach me at this number, or at my e-mail address. Have a great day."

When Tiana heard that message, his voice sent a warm and sexual sensation throughout her body. He had such an enchanting accent that she started to picture him as a sexy, tall, and handsome gentleman and a valuable client. She returned his call. In two weeks, they would meet.

Early Friday morning, Harry arrived in New York, rented a car and drove to Tiana's agency. When she saw him, he enchanted her. He was the most handsome man she had ever seen. He introduced himself, took her hand and kissed it.

She broke out in goose bumps. For her, it was love at first sight. If getting back at Dafoe was her number one aim in life, that intent went to the back burner. She was now on planet longing, and Dafoe became a distant haze.

Harry knew then that he had her completely under his sway and was ready to put his malicious scheme into motion.

Finding a place to accommodate his business was Harry's main objective. He explained to Tiana that a house with an office would be the ideal setting and stressed,

"There must be enough space to entertain and hold meetings with my business associates and backers. I will be traveling to New York often to seek sponsors for the construction of my second hotel in Tunisia. My country is a great tourist attraction with marvelous beaches, beautiful backdrops, and great investment opportunities. Last year, revenues from my hotel were over two hundred million dollars. So, money is no object when it comes to purchasing a home."

Tiana was paying special attention to him, as if she were a student listening to her teacher. To say she was love-struck with Harry was clear-cut. She quickly got down to business. Selecting several homes, in some of the most exclusive areas in Suffolk County, would be her main intent.

She invited him out to dinner to get a better feel for the type of house that would best meet his needs, but she also wanted to know more about this man, because she was attracted to him, as a shark would be to blood.

Later that evening, Tiana took Harry to a restaurant at the country club. He started to talk about his life growing up in Tunisia.

His mother died after giving birth to him, and his father, who went into the hotel business as a young man, raised him.

When his father died, Harry took over the hotel, which was a popular spot because of its location near the seaport of Tunis, the capital of Tunisia.

While he was talking, Dafoe and Hope walked into the restaurant.

Tiana then grabbed Harry's hand to make Dafoe jealous and had a beam on her face that read, *Look at me now. I have a new man in my life, and I am doing very well without you; eat your heart out, you good for nothing!*

Dafoe looked at her, as though he had just lost his best friend and disappeared with his wife into a private dining room.

After dinner, Tiana invited Harry to her home to converse more.

After entering her house, he loved it and said, "A place like this would be ideal. How much would a home like this cost?" he asked.

She answered, "A little over four million dollars."

"Well, if you can find a house like this, that would be great," he said.

In an eager pitch, she replied, "I'll get on it first thing in the morning and have some showings for you on Monday."

In the meantime, she offered him a drink. They continued to talk. She mentioned how she got into the real estate business. The two had so much in common.

Their parents were business owners, and Tiana and Harry inherited that entrepreneurial spirit. He was looking for financiers, and she was seeking to expand her horizons, financially and romantically. They agreed that combining their resources would be a great business undertaking.

The talk of money and business started to turn her on. She invited him to spend the night. They ran into the bedroom, undressed each other and made love like two horny squirrels in the playing field. He had more moves than a sumo wrestler did. She could not get enough of him.

He was so intoxicating that when he retreated, she took over. In her erotic state, she grabbed on to him like a leech, and he responded with his dazzling moves. After hours of deep sex, the two took a thirty-minute break and subsequently went for a second round, with no hiatus in sight. At first, she thought he was on a sex enhancement drug. What other explanation was there that allowed him to do her for over four hours.

I wasted six years of my being with Dafoe, the dud, who never even measured up to this man. Being dumped by him was the best move he could have ever made, she thought.

After the great spine tingling climax, she was ready to be Harry's lover and business partner for life and was no longer going to waste her energy destroying Dafoe.

It was around noon when Harry woke up. He got out of bed, took a shower and dressed. Tiana was already up. He kissed her and gave thanks for a breathtaking night. As he was getting ready to leave, his cell phone rang. It was a business associate calling from abroad.

"Hello, Mr. Ubey, it is great hearing from you. I am in New York, looking for a house. Yes, I am still seeking investors. Are you still interested in my proposal? Good, I will get back to you shortly. Bye."

By now, Tiana ears grew longer than Pinocchio's nose; she became more infatuated with Harry and would meet with him at her office, later that day.

At her headquarters, Tiana met with Harry. She wanted to know more about his business venture.

He went on to explain, "I plan to build a hotel not too far from my other one. It will be a fashionable intercontinental hotel, with five hundred rooms and all the amenities fit for a dignitary. Rooms will start at one thousand dollars per night. The cost to construct this hotel will be approximately thirty-five million dollars. So far, I have raised twenty-five million and have a commitment of five million dollars from a business associate in Ghana. I plan to meet with him next Sunday. This is why it is important for me to find a house before I leave New York."

He showed her the prospectus, which included the estimated expenditures for supplies, and workers, projected sales, and the percentage of returns that investors would receive.

"The construction will begin in several months and should be completed in two years," he said.

She did not need to hear any more of his sales pitch, wanted in and said, "I have the five million dollars to complete the deal. Just tell me what to do next."

"I will give you my bank account number and let you know when and where to wire the funds," he responded.

Tiana found the perfect home for Harry. Designed with the home-based businessperson in mind, the beautiful mansion was 6,000 square feet and came with six bedrooms, six baths, a large dining area and living room, three fireplaces, a conference room, and a state-of-the art office. The estate stood on three acres of land and included a swimming pool, sauna, golf course, tennis court, and a spectacular fishpond.

She contacted Harry. He came to her office, and they went to see the house. She gave him the majestic tour; he fell in love with the place and said, "You are a psychic; this is exactly what I had in mind, and it will definitely serve my needs."

Her asking price was four million dollars. He accepted her bid.

Being so overjoyed, they celebrated and made love for the remaining day.

While in heated bliss, he whispered, "When I walked into your office that first day, I immediately fell in love with you. Will you marry me?"

"Yes! Yes! Yes!" she yelled from the top of her lungs. Accepting his marriage proposal was the ultimate sexual peak for her.

To meet with Mr. Ubey, Harry was leaving on a Friday evening flight to Ghana. On his way to the airport, he made a quick stop to Tiana's house and gave her his account number. He watched her as she went online and wired five millions dollars into his account. He then handed her a certified check for four million dollars, gave her a big hug and a peck on the cheek and said, "I will be back in six weeks, and I already miss you."

She said, "Have a safe trip, my love. I'll be waiting for you."

He got into his rental car and took off for the airport.

First thing Monday morning, Tiana called the society editor of the Sag Harbor Weekly and took out the following full-page announcement:

Mr. and Mrs. Henry Bates would like to announce the engagement of their daughter, Ms. Tiana Bates, to Mr. Harry Goto, a prominent Tunisian hotelier. The marriage will take place next year.

The news about Tiana's engagement traveled faster than a thoroughbred racing to the finish line at the Kentucky Derby. When the community read that notice, the talk was non-stop. She was receiving calls from serious and so-called well-wishers.

The country club called inquiring if the couple was planning to have an engagement party, and if so, the VIP room would be the ideal place to hold the event.

People who never spoke to her were suddenly showing an interest in her fiancé. A major hotel owner in a foreign country was very enticing and perhaps a great place to invest or hide one's money.

When Hope read the news, she was delighted and expected that Tiana would be moving to Tunisia with Harry and away from Dafoe.

Tiana called her parents and shared the good news about her engagement to Harry. She talked about how they met and had fallen in love.

Several days later, she went to the bank and deposited his check into her business account. As she was leaving the bank, Dafoe, looking so down in the dumps, approached her and offered his best wishes, but in a smug manner, she ignored him as though he were just a dust bunny on the floor.

For the next four weeks, Tiana was gobbling up land and homes at foreclosure auctions, like an uncontrollable greedy gut. As she was getting ready to leave her office, the phone rang. It was the bank informing her that the four million dollar check, which she deposited a month ago, was a fake.

Tiana thought the caller was a prankster and hung up.

The bank called back and reiterated, "The check is a counterfeit; do not hang up, or you will be receiving a visit from law enforcement."

In a cocky tone, Tiana said, "It is not bogus. The check was written by a reputable businessman and drawn on a USA bank in Tunisia!"

The spokesperson restated, "Trust me, the check is not authentic. The bank in Tunisia never issued that check, which lacked the hidden watermark that would have identified the instrument as genuine. Furthermore, there is no record of a Mr. Harry Goto having an account at that bank. While this matter is under investigation, the bank has frozen all of your accounts."

In a naive tone, Tiana asked, "What about the money I wired into Mr. Goto's account?"

The woman put Tiana on hold, came back and said, "The money was deposited into an offshore account in Asuncion, Paraguay, but the account was closed three weeks ago."

When Tiana got off the phone, she started to shake as though some satanic force had taken over her body. As she tried to get up from her desk, she fell back into the chair and started to sob, uncontrollably.

Her phone was ringing, and fuming customers were leaving nasty messages regarding her bounced checks, but she did not return the calls. She sat there in a daze and understood that Harry had stolen her life's savings.

It was ironic, because history had repeated itself. Dafoe used her, but at least she received financial rewards. Harry exploited her, and he became five million dollars richer.

The bank placed a lien on her agency, home, and other assets. The state revoked her real estate broker's license, and there was the likelihood that she would be facing criminal charges.

The news about Tiana's financial mess did not take long to reach the communities that she served. Many could not believe that a stranger conned an astute woman out of her money. Some of her former co-workers felt she got just what she deserved, because she was a conniving barracuda in her business dealings, which in the end destroyed her.

Some members of the country club thought she was too busy attempting to be a wannabe aristocrat and bit off more than she could chew. No matter how hard she tried, she could never be one of them.

At times, the gossip was vicious. At social events, Tiana was the only subject matter when it came to conversations. Yet, many felt relieved that they did not jump the gun and invest their money into her fiancé's business project.

Ultimately, Tiana lost everything. Her home, agency and properties were auctioned off. The bank did not bring any criminal charges against her. It was apparent that she was an innocent victim of Harry's cruel scheme.

Her staying in New York was no longer affordable. Too broke and embarrassed to remain in Sag Harbor, she decided to move to St. Lucia to be with her family. No one from the community saw or heard from her again.

In the end, the talk died down, and Tiana became the woman who once had it all but was too foolish to hold on to what she had accrued.

A year later, Harry was living somewhere in the South Pacific. While online at an Internet café, he received the following e-mail:

Dear Harry:

The balance of your payment has been wired into your account. Again, thank you for the excellent role you played in destroying that trifling excuse of a woman, who brought nothing but shame to our community. When I hired you and provided you with the history of this woman, I knew she would fall for the two enticements: Money and sex. Now, she is gone, and things are back to normal. Stay well, and enjoy your new established wealth. There will be no more contacts between us. Thanks again, and best wishes to you.

With a big smile on his face, Harry deleted the message, closed his e-mail account and left for parts unknown. Wherever he was going, the one million dollars he received from Hope Tang would be waiting for him at an undisclosed bank account.■

<u>Crossing Paths</u>

Harry Goto was now living in Roseau, the capital of Dominica. When he first arrived on the island, three years ago, he had six million dollars.

With some of that money, he purchased a split-level home with four steps leading up to two bedrooms, two baths, a fully fitted kitchen, and a roomy dining area. The bedrooms had built-in wardrobes, chest drawers, twelve feet ceilings, and tiled floors.

A spacious lounge led into an enclosed terrace. Other amenities included a utility and laundry room, cable TV, digital phone system, DSL Internet connection, and panoramic views of the mountainsides and the Caribbean Sea. He paid one hundred and fifty thousand dollars for the property.

As a silent partner, he invested close to two hundred and fifty thousand dollars into a thriving tour guide business that catered to hikers, nature-lovers, snorkeling enthusiasts, and scuba divers.

The island, with its population of approximately seventy thousand, was the ideal environment for honeymooners, retirees, and folks looking for serenity, untouched nature, and friendly people. Crime was nearly non-existent, and people went about their daily routines with very little time for idle gossiping or meddling into other people's affairs. Soon that would all change. An avalanche of deceit and the settling of old scores were about to boil over on the tiny island. If the inhabitants were craving for some unusual excitement, their wish was about to come true.

Down the road was another estate, similar to Harry's home. He would pass the property but never noticed anyone moving about and assumed the house was unoccupied. Every night, the place was completely dark. He figured that the owner was holding on to the residence, would eventually flip it and make a nice return on his investment.

Meanwhile, Tiana had gotten her life back on track. She was still living in Saint Lucia, had her own condominium and a lucrative job selling time-shares for an online company called Oceanside Realty Ltd., which owned some of the most lavish and expensive estates on the island. Most of their properties were located on secluded beaches and offered picturesque views of the ocean and mountainsides, which were great enticements for wealthy vacationers.

Over a three-year period, she accumulated nearly three hundred and fifty thousand dollars from commissions and referrals. It was now time for her to take a long-awaited and well-deserved vacation. She considered visiting Sag Harbor, but the ache of what Defoe and Harry had done to her was still fresh in her mind.

She often wondered if Dafoe ever thought about her while he was making love to his wife. There were times when she wanted to call him, just to hear his voice. She even thought about writing a letter of apology for the way she treated him at the bank that day, but those were just idle thoughts.

Her inner voice would always keep asking, *Why are you having these feelings and putting yourself through such pain, yet again?*

Oceanside Realty Ltd. was planning to expand their operations on other islands in the Caribbean, one of them being Dominica. Since Tiana was one of their top agents, the company e-mailed her and asked if she would be interested in traveling to the isle and staying at one of their recently purchased properties. They wanted her opinion as to whether the place would make a profitable time-share. The firm would pay for all travel expenses and meals. The offer came at a good time.

Since she was planning to take a break, she e-mailed her decision. *Yes, I will gladly take the trip, stay at the estate and e-mail my feedback to you.* In two weeks, she would leave and remain there for one week.

Tiana received a round-trip plane ticket and a travel itinerary that included a map, information on the island, a restaurant and shopping guide, and sites of interests. She would leave Saint Lucia on Friday morning and arrive at her destination at noon. A car would be waiting to take her to the estate. But due to inclement weather, her plane did not leave St. Lucia until Saturday afternoon and landed in Dominica early that evening. The driver was at the airport and drove her to the house.

The exterior of the place was beautiful and reminded her of the home she once had in Sag Harbor. While touring the estate, her mind went back to Dafoe and the times they spent making attention-grabbing love in those empty for-sale mansions. When she walked into the master bedroom, her body became hot, and sensual thoughts were inundating her head. Suddenly, the phone rang. It was the reality company checking to make certain she had arrived safely. After getting off the phone, she decided to unpack and take a thirty-minute nap.

When Tiana woke up, it was Sunday morning. She dashed out of the bed, took a shower, dressed and decided to have breakfast at a local café. As she looked out the window to take in the beautiful countryside, her heart started to skip beats, and her head felt like it was ready to explode. At first, she thought she was dreaming, but she was not; it was really him, Harry Goto, strolling down the street as though he did not have a care in the world. The shock of seeing him was incredible. For her, it was like watching the popular TV series: Ripley's Believe It or Not!

What a small world. The likelihood of running into him is one in a million. Now I understand why the company sent me here. It is to exact retribution on that evil son of a gun. If it is the last endeavor I carry out, he will regret the day he crossed me, she thought.

Before leaving, Tiana decided to wait and see if Harry would walk by the estate again; if he did, she would follow him. Waiting patiently, she sat by the window. An hour later, he appeared. To disguise herself, she wore a big floppy straw hat and dark sunglasses; she left the house and followed him.

Lo and behold, he entered the house that was on the same road where she was staying. She ran past his house and went into a nearby café. She had to get her wits together and find out if he were a tourist, tenant, or the owner of that house. If he were vacationing, she would have to act fast and put together a plan that would ruin him. Besides, she only had one week to compose a workable line of attack that would not come back and bite her in the butt.

As she sat there contemplating her next move, a woman walked in and ordered coffee and a croissant. The coffee shop was jam-packed with locals and tourists, and the only seat available was at Tiana's table.

The woman came over and asked, "Excuse me, is this seat taken?"

"No, please sit down," Tiana answered.

"Thank you," said the woman, who then asked, "Are you a tourist, or do you live here?"

"No, I live in Saint Lucia. I am here on an assignment for my company. I am staying at the estate on Battery Road and studying the property to see if it would be viable as a time-share for vacationers. My name is Tiana. Could you please tell me if the house down the road is up for sale or if anyone lives there? I think my employer might be interested in purchasing that property. They are planning to expand their business here and throughout the Caribbean Islands."

By now, the woman showed an intense interest in Tiana's work and said, "That sounds great, and my name is Paradise, and I have lived on this island for several years, and the house you are referring to belongs to Mr. Harry Goto. He is also a partner in a tour guide company. Because he keeps mostly to himself, not too much is known about him."

Acting like a clueless woman, Tiana said, "Gee, I once knew a man who went by that name, and he betrayed me in such a horrific way. I wonder if this is the same person, and if so, there will be hell to pay."

As the women continued to talk, Harry walked into the café to order take-out.

Paradise saw him and whispered, "This is your lucky day. Harry Goto just walked in and is at the counter."

Tiana slowly turned around. Acting stunned, she said, "Oh my goodness, that's him! That's Harry Goto! I can't believe he's here!" When Harry left the café, Tiana went into details about what he had done to her.

Paradise was extremely fascinated with her story. After all, she was one of the greatest manipulators when it came to conning men out of their money and offered to assist

Tiana in getting back at him but only if she were willing to split whatever amount of money Paradise could get from Harry.

Tiana thought about it and decided to work with her. They agreed to meet at a clandestine place. There were many out-of-the-way beaches in Dominica, and since Tiana did not know her way around the island, she had to rely on Paradise to find a spot where they could meet and put together a scheme that would obliterate Harry.

Because Dominica was a tiny island, just about everyone knew everybody, either casually or officially. Therefore, Paradise came up with a brilliant idea. She would ingratiate herself into Harry's life by pretending to be an interested homebuyer for a business associate living abroad and play on his greed and arrogance.

In order for the plan to be successful, they would have to work fast. Tiana thought the plot was perfect and gave Paradise the okay to proceed.

Since Harry would recognize Tiana, she had to keep a low profile. Paradise suggested that she leave the estate and check into a remote inn.

Tiana felt that was a splendid suggestion, because she had already concluded that the estate would make a profitable time-share. With its structural design, great amenities, and proximity to the city, airport, and other sites of interest, the house would be a magnet for wealthy travelers.

She went back to the estate, packed her bags, called a cab and checked into a motel that Paradise had recommended. All Tiana had to do now was wait for the scenario to unfold.

When his doorbell rang, Harry had just gotten out of the shower. With a towel wrapped around him, he opened the door and stood there as though he was ready to take a trip to the land of sexual gratification.

"Good morning, I hope I did not disturb you. My name is Paradise, and I live on the other side of Battery Road, have strolled past your beautiful home on many occasions and would like to know if you are interested in selling the property. I have a business associate living in Europe, and he is planning, along with his family, to relocate here and would be willing to offer you top dollars for your estate."

If Harry was listening to her, it was not noticeable. He was excessively sizing her up and down and calculating how he was going to get her into his bed. Holding back the dribble in his mouth and trying to control his lust demons were proving to be quite hard for him. He invited her in, introduced himself and apologized for not being decent.

"I just came out of the shower. Excuse me while I put on some clothes, and please, make yourself at home," he said with a look of hunger in his eyes.

She knew then that he was under her command.

While Harry was getting dress, he was thinking, *What a beauty. How did I miss seeing her on this island, and where on the other side does she live? I thought I knew most of the women in this area. She must have just moved here. I cannot wait to see more of her. It will be just a matter of time before she starts lusting for my body.*

He came out of the bedroom, sat on the love seat and wanted to know everything about this woman, but she steered the conversation back to his house.

"I am familiar with most of the houses in this neighborhood, because they have similar interior and exterior designs. As I mentioned, I have an associate who is interested in purchasing a home. Since he is a person of means, money is not a problem."

Before she could continue, Harry interrupted her and said, "Perhaps your friend would be interested in the house down the road. I never see anyone in that place."

Her quick response was, "Oh, you probably didn't hear, but rumor has it that the property was purchased by a time-share corporation. I do not know the name of the company, but apparently, there is a need for such a venue, because the island lacks large hotels that would attract more visitors. Just think of the revenues that such a business could generate."

Harry sat there, pretending to be engrossed in her dialogue, but his only interest was to get her into his boudoir and make outrageous love to her.

Pretending to be serious about Paradise's offer, Harry said, "I might be interested in selling my home if the price is right."

She said, "Make an offer."

He said, "My asking price is five hundred thousand dollars for the house, and if he is interested in buying my share of the tour guide business, that will be one million dollars. I will gladly provide you with the prospectus outlining the company's returns for the last three years." If he thought she was going to concede to defeat because of his high asking price, Harry did not know Paradise.

Her response was, "I will get in touch with my friend, present him with your two bids and come by tomorrow evening, around eight, with his decision. In the meantime, if you don't mind, I would like to videotape your estate and e-mail the clip to him."

The taping took about two hours. She recorded every nook and cranny and took note of his laptop, which had an attached wireless Internet access card. She was now ready to put her malicious strategies into full gear.

Later that evening, Paradise met with Tiana at a remote shoreline to discuss Harry's two offers.

Paradise explained, "I know Harry is not serious about selling his home or his share of the tour guide business. All he wanted to do was get into my panties. I will meet with him tomorrow evening and inform him that both of his proposals were accepted, and the prospective buyer will offer him a large amount of cash as a down payment.

Harry will play along, because it is a game to him, and most likely, he will have something up his sleeve. However, I will be two steps ahead of him. For you, I have put together a list of offshore banks in countries that have no extradition treaties with Saint Lucia. It is important to select at least two of these depositories, open an account at each one and use a dummy corporation as a front. Once you get your money into one bank, wait awhile; close that account and move the money into your second account. If necessary, have a third account as a backup, so you will not leave a paper trail. When you open your accounts, do it online and at an Internet café. Never use your home computer or personal laptop when transferring large sums of money."

Tiana was familiar with offshore banking and knew exactly what to do. The next day, she went to an Internet café and opened an account in two different countries; she would then deposit a set amount of money into each bank.

On the following evening, at approximately 8 PM, Harry's doorbell rang. This time, he was fully clad. When he opened the door, there stood Paradise wearing a green sheer dress and animal print stilettos. It was obvious to him that she was not wearing any underwear.

Carrying a basket filled with mouth-watering treats, she sashayed into his home and said, "Good evening darling. I have great news. My associate saw the clip, immediately fell in love with your home and has accepted your two bids. To show good faith, he will wire five hundred thousand dollars into your account at once and the remaining one million dollars when both titles are signed over to him."

Harry was stunned and suspicious. He never believed the individual would accept his two offers. It sounded almost too good to be true. *What person in their right mind would purchase an estate for that amount of money, when most of the homes on this road can be purchased for as little as two hundred and fifty thousand dollar*, he thought.

Just as she anticipated, he declined the two offers and said, "You can thank your associate for his generosity, but I have decided not to sell my home or my share in the tour guide company. I plan to turn my estate into a lodge and give that time-share business down the road some stiff competition."

Her response was, "That sounds like a great idea. I have some delicious munchies and a bottle of sparkling wine in my basket. Let us celebrate your new business initiative, get comfortable and enjoy the remaining evening."

She excused herself, went into the bathroom, removed her dress and applied a dab of Egyptian Musk oil behind her ears, on her breasts, and in between her legs. Naked as a jade bird, she came back into the living room.

Harry was like a horny tomcat ready to ambush a pussy in heat. He quickly removed his clothes and was ready to get down, but she stopped him and whispered, "I am ravenous; let's eat first."

He surrendered and began consuming the food, as though it was his last meal. She then poured him a drink. He quickly drank the wine, picked her up and carried her into the bedroom. As he started to get on top of her, the room started to spin, and he passed out. She quickly dressed, searched his laptop, found the user name, password, and pin number to his online bank account.

It was close to midnight when she called Tiana, told her to come to the house immediately and not to worry about

Harry recognizing her, because he was dead to the world and would not come around for hours. Fifteen minutes later, Tiana was at Harry's estate and made certain no one saw her enter his house.

When Paradise logged on to his account, it had four million dollars. She also discovered that he was embezzling and transferring money from the tour guide company's account into a secret account, which had another six million dollars.

From both accounts, she moved half of the money into her offshore account, and Tiana wired the other half between her two bank accounts. Paradise installed software that closed his two accounts and wiped out all transactions that took place on his laptop.

They drove Harry to a secluded beach and left him there, along with his notebook. The women drove back to the inn where Tiana was staying. Before getting out the car, she hugged and thanked Paradise for her help. The women agreed never to meet or contact each other.

The next morning, Tiana checked out of the motel. There was no need for her to remain in Dominica. She accomplished her mission and unexpectedly killed three birds with one stone, the stone being Paradise and the birds being Harry and his two bank accounts. She e-mailed her report, outlining her positive comments, to Oceanside Realty, was able to get a flight out late that afternoon and arrived in St. Lucia early that evening. She was as happy as a puma that just eradicated a rat.

In the meantime, Paradise was planning to leave the island, not that she ever lived there. Like Tiana, she was vacationing there, which she had done for the past two years. She knew about Harry, because she would hear the islanders warning individuals about him, because he was a shady character. In another life, the two might have become kindred spirits.

When she turned in her rental car, the agent said, "Thank you for using our service. We hope you enjoyed your stay on our beautiful island and look forward to serving you again. Have a safe trip home."

She turned and said, "Thank you, I will see you next year." She was on an evening flight to God knows where and would never return to Dominica.

The next morning, Harry woke up on the beach surrounded by gawking spectators. Many women and men were definitely impressed with his well-endowed twig.

People were asking, "Sir, are you all right."

Harry did not respond, because he could not remember who or where he was. He slowly got up and started to stumble along the path.

Someone yelled, "Put some clothes on." Harry stood there as though he could not comprehend what the person said and went under the footpath to get out of the sun. It was a cool day, and the time he spent on the coast did not create any blisters on his body.

After sitting on the seaside for almost an hour, his memory was slowly coming back; he remembered being with a woman named Paradise but could not explain how he ended up on the beach naked and with his laptop. All of a sudden, a little birdie said, *Go online and check your bank balance*. He went on the Internet, tried to log on to his account but got the following message: Access denied. You no longer have an account at this bank.

In shock, he screamed, "Paradise stole my money." With tears streaming down his face, he continued to call her name and yelled, "I will hunt you down like the wicked person you are! You will not get away with this or live in peace."

He got up and frantically ran along the shoreline, shouting and acting like a deranged man. He dived in and out of the water, as if he were a dolphin entertaining the crowd. For almost an hour, he kept repeating, "Paradise, Paradise, I am coming for you," as though she were a mermaid immersed under the sea. It was as if some demonic spirit had taken over his body.

People were looking on in complete horror. Some thought he was attempting to drown himself. Many locals and tourists were recording the incident on their camcorders or taking pictures with their digital cameras and cell phones. Eventually, someone called the police, and Harry was arrested for indecent exposure and creating a public nuisance.

Within minutes, the scandal erupted throughout the island faster than lava spurting out of a volcano; the incidence aired on the evening news. Video clips of the event started to appear on several social networking sites, including a popular video streaming site, which got over two million hits.

According to reports, Harry claimed that a woman named Paradise, who lived across the road from his house, seduced and drugged him. She kidnapped him, along with his laptop, got into his bank account, stole his money and dumped him on the beach.

Folks on the island were puzzled. No one knew of a woman named Paradise. With such a beautiful first name, the residents on the other side of Battery Road would have surely known her.

The story did not end there. The islanders discovered that Harry was pilfering money from the tour guide business. The talk was that he used his laptop to hack into the company's bank account, removed all of the money and then closed his accounts, but no one had a clue as to where the funds went. Not even law enforcement could track or find the stolen money.

In the end, Harry went on trial. The court found him guilty of embezzling millions of dollars from the company and sentenced him to twenty-five years in prison. The tour guide business went out of business.

A year later, people were still talking about Harry and that so-called Paradise. Most people believed his guilt got the best of him, and the woman was a figment of his distorted imagination.

Many of the locals lost their jobs because of him, and some businesses suffered financially since their source of income relied heavily on the tour guide's clientele.

The old saying: *What goes around comes around* played out very well against him, but at the same time, many innocent people were hurt.

Every night, he complained to the guards, asserting that Paradise would sneak into his cell and attempt to suffocate him with a pillow. He even claimed that she would place duck tape over his mouth and a plastic bag over his head and try to murder him with her bare hands. He would fight her off, but she would always return and attempt to take his life. He then accused her of lacing his food and drinks with cyanide and arsenic.

Fearing for his life, he pleaded with the magistrate to move him to another prison and away from Paradise's evil domination. Six months later, he was transferred to a psychiatric facility for the criminally insane.

Back in St. Lucia, Tiana opened a third offshore account at a bank that was not on Paradise's list. She moved all of her money from the two accounts and then closed them.

Based on her advice, the house where she stayed at in Dominica became a lucrative time-share. She also suggested that Oceanside Realty Ltd. acquire Harry Goto's estate. They took her advice and paid two hundred and fifty thousand dollars for the property. For her diligence and excellent job, she received a referral fee of twenty-five thousand dollars. One year later, she opened her own real estate agency, which became an immediate success. Once again, she was a member of the elite inner circle.

Paradise was now living in Sidney, Australia. Before arriving on that continent, she had more plastic surgery on her face. Her beautiful facade had men pursuing her as if she were the last woman on earth. She would have been just another pretty face in the crowd if Harry or Tiana bumped into her. Since Destiny Love was the name she used when visiting Dominica, it was now clear why no one on the island knew a woman named Paradise.■

Blind Faith

After taking over House of Fashions, Faith Bell's vision of becoming a leader in the couture world was starting to happen. When several banks denied her a business loan, she did not allow the setback to prevent her from meeting her goals and was determined to make the company one of the most successful houses in the fashion industry.

House of Fashions was the brainchild of Faith's mother, who started the business after her husband of one year died suddenly.

Faith's parents met in church, and six months later, they were married. Three months after Faith was born, her father was gone. Her mother rarely talked about him or the circumstances under which he died. As a child, Faith would hear stories about her dad, but they were all unconfirmed reports that came from strangers, neighbors, church members, and distant relatives.

The rumor mill was that he was having an affair with the minister's wife, and someone had placed a hex on her father, but no one knew who ordered the curse: The minister or her mother. There was also talk that her father had a mistress, but not a soul knew who or where she was. The ultimate tale was that he had another wife, and she was living somewhere in Central America. Soon, these claims became mute.

Left with mounting bills, no source of income, and a child to rear, her mother would dismiss those talks as idle gossip by folks who had nothing better to do than to meddle into other people's business and started to concentrate on putting her designing talents to work.

While growing up, Faith would watch her mother, who ran the business from a two-bedroom apartment in the

Wallabout section of Brooklyn, New York, make some of the most stunning outfits. Her mother never had any formal training in pattern making, sketching, or sewing, but everything she made came naturally. She could look at any design in a magazine, make a pattern and stitch those samples into something amazing. Her customers included friends, relatives, neighbors, and church members. Moreover, it did not take long for her daughter to inherit her mother's talents, and in no time, Faith was coming up with unique creations of her own.

After graduating from high school, Faith attended a renowned fashion and design institute in Manhattan. She took courses in pattern making, draping, sketching, merchandising, retailing, and business management. If House of Fashions had any prospects of becoming competitive and financially sound, she would have to concentrate more on the business end, which her mother overlooked.

There were times when her mother would extend credit to customers, but to collect those payments was like trying to extract molars from a rhinoceros. The excuses given were always the same: "I will pay you when I get my income tax refund. I am short this week. The raise or promotion that was promised to me fell through."

Some customers would deliberately start arguments or find fault with the garments just to avoid paying what they owed. It was a never-ending battle, demanding monies from people who were wearing the finished product that her mother spent tedious hours and sometimes weeks to make. It got to the point where the business was operating at a loss, and this is when Faith stepped in and took over.

Right from the start, problems were looming after Faith took over the business. When it came to managing the company, she and her mother were constantly at odds. Two years later, they had a falling-out.

Her mother left New York for Barbados, where she was born and started to design clothes for local boutiques, wealthy patrons, and tourists. Her business became such a success that she was able to purchase a house with an attached loft, which became a fashion production company called Grandeur Couture. She continued to make the patterns and hired local homemakers to cut and piece the fabrics together.

In five years, her mother's business made over one million dollars in profits. Even though the two kept in touch, the relationship started to wither. House of Fashions was still operating at a deficit. Faith became somewhat resentful of her mother's success and eventually ceased communicating with her.

While Faith concentrated on designing, she hired a part-time consultant to manage the financial and business elements of the company. It took three years for House of Fashions to break even. Still operating from her Brooklyn apartment, she narrowed her scope to cocktail dresses and evening gowns.

Most of her customers came through word-of-mouth, but a positive write-up, in a community newspaper, gave her business a much-needed boost. Her designs were beginning to take the media and the fashion world by storm. More articles were emerging in high fashion and women's publications.

She even appeared on a popular cable program called *Today's Style*, which reached over five million viewers and was a frequent guest on the radio talk show, *Conversations with Tea,* whose listeners tuned in from the Tri-State Region.

Orders for her dresses and gowns were coming in faster than she could produce. Major department stores and high-end clothing shops were ordering her creations as though they were going out of style. Working from her apartment was no longer viable, and filling orders became more of a challenge.

Her business consultant suggested that Faith would have to obtain a line of credit in order to hire a team of workers, buy more production equipment and find larger quarters to work from, or the business would suffer and eventually fail.

Before applying for a business loan, Faith had to put together a mission statement, which included a five-year business and financial plan, marketing, operating and management costs, reasons for the loan, and why the bank should lend her money.

This project was not going to be an easy task and would soon prove costly. Even though she took courses in business management, the lessons she learned never prepared her for what was about to transpire in the real world.

As far as resources were concerned, she had two thousand dollars in an IRA, one thousand dollars in savings, and three thousand dollars in her checking account. The business account had over two hundred and fifty thousand dollars from the orders for her designs. She projected that one million dollars would cover the leasing of commercial space, purchasing equipment and hiring sewers and pattern makers.

She would utilize students, majoring in clothing design; their work experiences would go toward college credits, and she would provide the interns with glowing letters of recommendations for potential employers.

After meeting with numerous banks, Faith did not get the loan. The reasons given for denying her financing were endless: You have no financial track record or collateral. The fashion industry is a risky and an erratic business. Most establishments fail during the first five to seven years. Even though you have been in the business for over ten years and have orders in the six figures, with the economy at its worst since the Great Depression, we are not in the position to take such a chance and lend money to a small business at the present time.

She thought the explanations were oxymoronic, because these same banks received billions of dollars in bailout money to help kick-start the economy and were supposed to lend some of that money to struggling small enterprises. With orders for her designs mounting, she was now at a stalemate and in desperate need of advice and money. While contemplating her next move, the phone rang.

On the other end was a man who said, "Good day, may I speak to Faith Bell? This is Troy Sooner calling."

"This is she," Faith answered.

He went on to explain, "I recently read an article about House of Fashions. I am a lawyer and would like to know more about you and your company. If you have any questions, please visit my web site at troysooner.bus."

She said, "What a stroke of luck that you would call me now. I am in desperate need of legal guidance and financial support and will definitely visit your site and get back to you. Thank you for calling."

"My pleasure," said the lawyer.

After getting off the phone, she went online to check his site. His web page, photo, and credentials were extremely impressive, and he was no doubt the most handsome man she had ever laid eyes on. She immediately called his office and made an appointment to meet with him the next day.

Troy's office was located in the Brooklyn Heights section of Brooklyn, New York. Like Faith's company, his business was also home-based. He worked out of a four-story townhouse.

When she approached his house, the sign in the window read, *Troy Sooner, Attorney at Law. Your Business Is Our Business*. She rang the bell, and when the door opened, there stood this enchanting man looking as though he was ready to pose for a fashion magazine.

The picture on his web site fails to do him justice, she thought. He was tall, alluring, and sexy. She could not figure out what it was about him that had her longing to hop into bed with this man and allowing him to have his way with her. A feeling of delight started to run up and down her spine.

He extended his hand to shake hers and said, "You must be Faith Bell. I am Troy Sooner. Please, come in."

In a blushing pitch, she said, "Thank you, Mr. Sooner, for agreeing to see me on such short notice."

"It's my pleasure, and please, call me Troy. Mr. Sooner sounds too reserved, which I am not."

They both laughed and got down to business.

She began to discuss her dilemma: "I was turned down by three banks for a loan and do not know how I am going to expand my business without financing. The requests for my designs are piling high, and I have been working non-stop to fill those orders."

She talked about how the business got started, the many problems her mother encountered when she started House of Fashions and how the company became successful when Faith took over.

He listened to her very attentively and made the following suggestions: "Your business should be set up as a corporation instead of a sole-proprietorship. As a corporate entity, you will have limited liabilities and protection from unforeseen suits and creditors, coming after your personal assets. If you plan to continue working from your apartment, you should have business in the home insurance. If you already have this type of coverage, increase your protection by fifty percent. I assume you have an accountant, if not I can recommend one to you. You will also need a power of attorney, authorizing someone to act on your behalf in signing legal documents and making authorized decisions in case you become incapacitated. Of course, a will must be drawn, designating who shall inherit your business, personal assets, and real properties; you will also have to appoint an executor to carry out your expressed wishes."

While she was listening to Troy, Faith thought about her mother, who started the business in 1976. She did not have the money to hire a lawyer or an accountant nor did she have a banker who would lend her money. The thought of having these experts in her life probably never crossed her mind.

An unforeseen tragedy forced her to put her God-given gifts to work. There was no time to put together a business plan, power of attorney, or a will. Like many self-employed people, she used credit cards to finance her business.

She was too busy putting food on the table, raising a daughter, being creative, extending credit to unappreciative customers and letting the financial end of the business fall along the way. Perhaps, this is why the business was failing.

For these reasons, Faith never wanted to be in that same predicament.

As Troy continued to talk, she was watching him like a hawk in heat. Burning with desire, her pupils started to dilate. After looking intensely at him for almost sixty seconds, she took control of herself and came back to earth.

Faith was extremely pleased with Troy's recommendations and gave him the go ahead to prepare and file all the necessary papers. She appointed him as her power of attorney and the executor of her will. His fee was twelve hundred dollars; she took out her checkbook and paid him.

With a shifty smile on his face, he thanked her and said, "I know a real estate broker who owns a private lending company; she provides loans to small businesses that have been denied financing by traditional banks. I will talk to her about your company and get back to you. We will then discuss locating a commercial space for your business."

When Faith left Troy's office, she was already missing him and was starting to have feelings, which she had never experienced before.

A drop-dead beauty is how most men saw her. She was petite, curvy, well put together, and the personification of true elegance. At age thirty-three, her perfect skin, well-toned body, and classy mannerisms were turning heads.

Work left her very little time to date or form a serious romantic relationship. Finding a man was never a problem, but her business always came first, which some men could not compete with or comprehend. But after meeting Troy, she was ready to make that commitment and saw the two of them working together as lovers and business partners. To her thinking, it was going to be a romantic match made in paradise.

When she got home, there was a message from him on her answering machine. He wanted to meet and discuss with her how she could get a quick loan for House of Fashions. She returned his call and would meet with him the following day.

As soon as Faith arrived at Troy's home, he was on his cell phone. Placing his hand over the speaker, he whispered to her, "This call is going to take about twenty minutes." He escorted her into the dining area, where fresh flowers and refreshments lined the decorative table. She decided to sit and wait for him before helping herself to the snacks. He finally joined her and began to discuss the financing of her company.

"I spoke to the lending corporation, and they will provide you with one million dollars at a variable rate, which will be set forth by the lender. However, there is one stipulation: You will have to sign over your business to them until you repay the loan, after which time the ownership of the company will revert to you. You will still have complete control running the day-to-day operations. If you are in agreement with these provisions, I will draw up the papers."

She saw no harm in signing over her company. Since she already had orders totaling six figures and anticipated sales would double in one year, her paying back the loan in a timely manner would not be a problem; she agreed to the terms. The loan contract would be ready in two days.

At Troy's home, Faith met the loan agent. They both carefully read the papers, asked a few questions, which were answered to their satisfaction and signed the contract. She received a check for the approved amount. The loan broker shook her hand, wished her luck and then left.

Faith and Troy went into the dining area where a bottle of champagne was on ice. The two passed on good wishes by toasting each other. Slow music was playing. They started to dance, became fiery, undressed each other and made passionate love on the dining room table. Eventually, they ended up in the bedroom to continue their erotic acts of happiness. She was sizzling tamale, and he was hard as a rock. Their bodies intertwined as one, as if they were two butterflies bumping each other. The awesome lovemaking lasted until dawn.

When Faith woke up the following day, it was near noon. She was on cloud nine. Troy came into the bedroom and kissed her. Her libido was in overdrive, and he was sexually energized. They made love again until two o'clock in the afternoon.

Before she left, he told her he got a call from the real estate broker who found a commercial building, and the agent would meet with them the next day.

After leaving his home, she stopped at the bank and deposited the check into her business account. She then hurried home and for the remaining afternoon daydreamed about Troy being a part of her life without end.

The next day, Faith met Troy and the broker inside of a one-story brick building, which came with all the equipment capable of producing hundreds of dresses a day.

Upgrades included electrical wiring, plumbing, and roofing, and there were no noticeable signs of any code violations.

A five-year lease at five thousand dollars a month was presented. Faith accepted the offer and would pay the first year's rent in advance.

The next day, the parties met and closed the deal. When the real estate agent received a check for sixty-thousand dollars, the broker handed Faith two keys to the building. Faith gave one key to Troy.

Now ready to put together a workforce, she posted help-wanted flyers on bulletin boards at student hangouts and at fashion design schools and colleges.

The grand opening of House of Fashions would take place in two weeks. Several pattern makers and sewers were hired and scheduled to come in and start production on thousands of orders, but then the unthinkable happened. One week before the opening, Faith received a call from Troy; he wanted to meet her at the site, because he had a surprise for her.

She could not wait to see him, quickly went to the building and went inside and looked around, but he was not there. She decided to do a walk through again and pinched herself to make certain it was real. Having a building to work from was always one of her goals. When Faith entered her spacious office, on the desk was a computer with a big red bow wrapped around it and a note that read:

Dear Faith:
This personal computer is my gift to you.
Love always,
Troy

So overwhelmed by his generosity, she sat down and started to weep for joy. When she turned on the computer and touched the keyboard, an electric shock passed through her body and knocked her to the floor. Being semi-conscious, she was able to gather enough strength to dial 911 from her cell phone. Within minutes, the paramedics arrived and rushed her to the hospital. She suffered severe external and internal injuries and would have to remain in the hospital for several weeks.

When the hospital called Troy, he quickly rushed to Faith's side.

Having power of attorney, he would have to make important decisions regarding her company while she recuperated and whispered, "Don't worry. I am on top of everything and will get down to business at once. I will ask the workers to come in immediately and make certain they fill all orders, even if it means working around the clock. I will also notify all of your vendors, customers, friends, and neighbors about your unfortunate accident. All you need to do is rest and get well." He blew her a kiss and left.

After leaving the hospital, Troy went straight to Faith's bank. When he checked her business account, it had over 1.5 million dollars.

What she did not realize was that the one million dollar check, which she received from the lending company, was a counterfeit. The phony check, drawn on a foreign bank, would take her bank weeks to detect.

He removed and wired all of the money from her business, IRA, savings, and personal checking accounts into his secret account. Two days later, he vanished.

During her stay in the hospital, Faith had several skin grafts. There were some signs of permanent tissue scarring and nerve damage.

She questioned why Troy had not come to visit her. Not hearing from him for nearly two weeks, she started to worry. She called his home, but his phone was not in service. She then dialed the real estate agent's office but got the following recording, *the number you are trying to reach is no longer in service*.

Getting in touch with her business consultant did not fare any better either, because she was on vacation and was not due back for another two weeks.

Faith asked the attending physician if she could leave the hospital.

The doctor said, "With the possibility of an infection setting in and other complications occurring, I would like you to remain in the hospital for another two weeks."

After the hospital released her, Faith went straight to her apartment. Before she could enter her building, a reporter stopped her and asked, "Where have you been, and why have you left your customers and merchants in limbo?"

She stood there in a state of confusion and explained, "I was in the hospital recovering from an accident. My lawyer is handling all of my business and personal affairs. You can contact him at his home-office for additional information, or you can go straight to my factory. As we speak, my workers are sewing and shipping the designs. Thank you for your concern." She gave the reporter both addresses.

The journalist scurried over to Troy Sooner's home-office, expecting to find the answers, but he was about to receive information that would be an explosive piece for his newspaper and a lead-in for the six o'clock news.

Within minutes, the reporter was ringing Troy's doorbell, but there was no answer. Seeing the sign in the window, he knew he had the right address. As he was about to leave, a middle-aged woman was coming out of the house next door; he approached her and inquired about the lawyer.

She said, "I just moved here six months ago. According to the neighbors, the lawyer who lived there died under mysterious circumstances, two years ago. The house has been vacant ever since, but the sign was never removed, which is a good deterrent against break-ins and squatters."

The journalist then said, "But that's strange, because a woman implied that this lawyer was handling her affairs while she was in the hospital. How could this be if he is deceased?"

"I can't answer that. Perhaps you have the wrong address, or maybe the woman you spoke to was discombobulated. Wait a minute, I do remember seeing a man and two women going in and out of that house about a month ago and assumed they were potential homebuyers."

With a bewildered look on his face, the reporter said, "Well, thank you for taking the time to answer my questions. Have a nice day."

"And you as well," replied the woman with a wary look.

The reporter then went to House of Fashions, but on the door was a notice that read: *This building is condemned.* He decided to go to the hall of records and discovered that Troy Sooner owned the townhouse, the condemned building, a lending company, and a real estate agency. Since this man was dead, and no will or probate was on file, the investigation came to a dead-end.

It did not take long for mayhem and scandal to hit House of Fashions. The phone in Faith's apartment was ringing day and night. Enraged merchants and frustrated customers were leaving messages inquiring about their orders and asking, "Where are our dresses and gowns? Why are you ignoring our calls? What kind of business are you running?"

Her neighbors, friends, and church members had no idea she was in the hospital. Troy was supposed to notify them, but he never did.

Rumors started to travel that Faith took the money and deposited it into an offshore account, and the building, which she was set to move into was about to be demolished.

It was also uncovered that her electric shock did not result from faulty wiring but from someone deliberately pouring water on the keyboard.

If she thought her life and business were in disarray, Faith was about to get the biggest shock of her life. When she opened her bank statement, it showed that someone had cleaned out all of her accounts, and the loan check, which she deposited, was bogus.

Bank officials had no idea where her money went, because Troy Sooner did a first-rate job at covering his tracks.

As the story broke about House of fashions, the media started to place a negative spin on what really happened. An article, in a daily newspaper, implied that Faith was in on the fraud right from the start. As smart as she was, the writer wrote, *How could she have been so easily tricked by this unscrupulous individual?*

Those who knew her chatted among themselves and pondered, "Was Faith ever ready to take over her mother's company? Her mother might not have been sophisticated when it came to business, but she would have never fallen for such a fast-talking snake in the grass charmer. Sadly, her daughter never became heir to such aptitudes when it came to scrutinizing men like Troy."

When the business consultant heard about the horrifying news, she could not comprehend why Faith did not confer with her first before meeting with Troy. Her advisor never even met the lawyer or knew about the loan or the leasing of the building. Since she was an independent contractor, her input into the business was at best minimal.

When she tried to call Faith, she kept getting a busy signal; finally, she went to her apartment, knocked on the door but never got an answer. She slipped a note under her door, asking Faith to contact her. Six months had gone by, but the consultant never heard from Faith.

Bank officials and the district attorney's office were investigating the phony check. The bank could not freeze anything, because there was nothing there to freeze. Faith had no personal or business assets to place liens on, and complaints and suits against her were growing. People requesting refunds were on the rise; suppliers receiving returned checks marked insufficient funds were after her like ants searching for food at a cookout.

Now that she was in dire financial straits, the news about her disastrous circumstances got back to her mother, who came to New York to be by her daughter's side. Their meeting was somewhat bittersweet. They had not spoken to each other for several years. Faith went into all the horrendous particulars that had occurred.

Her mother just sat there in total disbelief, but in a non-judgmental tone asked, "What can I do to help?"

After all, her mother was young and impressionable when she met and married Faith's father. *Falling in love can cloud one's judgment*, her mother surmised.

After consulting with an attorney, who negotiated a deal between the bank and the district attorney, Faith would not face any criminal charges. It was quite apparent that she was unknowingly a sitting duck for one of the cruelest cons ever perpetrated. Because Troy never incorporated her business, Faith was personally responsible for all debts. Her mother took care of that and paid all parties concerned, which was a little over two million dollars.

A year later, Faith decided to leave New York with her mother for Barbados. While on the plane, her mind went back to the first day she met Troy. For her, it was love at first vision. She fell hard for him. So in lust, she never saw the in your face warnings: His contacting her out of the blue, his haste to become her power of attorney and executor of her will, and his affiliation with a company that was too eager to give her a loan and lease her a building without checking her credit history.

Looking back, the events were all too good to be true. She then recognized that Troy was trying to get rid of her for good.

When the plane landed in Bridgetown, the capitol of Barbados, Faith and her mother got a cab and went straight home. Her mother's estate stunned Faith.

The property rested on three acres of land and had a breathtaking pool, sauna, and a carriage house. Behind the house was Grandeur Couture's production site and showroom.

After entering the two-story house, Faith became even more flabbergasted. The lower level had an open living room, a state-of-the art gourmet kitchen, and a spacious dining area. On the second level were three large bedrooms, three full baths, and a powder room for guests. It was obvious to Faith that her mother had done extremely well and learned from her past mistakes.

After unpacking, Faith took a hot bath and again, thought about Troy. She gathered that he was somewhere doing what he does best: Getting women to trust and fall in love with him, conning them out of their money and then plotting their demise. She was lucky; the gods were watching over her.

Getting out of the tub, she dressed and joined her mother for dinner. The two had a long conversation about the future and Faith's position in her mother's company. It was quite clear that as long as her mother was alive and able-bodied, Faith was never going to take over Grandeur Couture but would continue to do what she does best:

Creating trendy cocktail dresses and elegant evening gowns.

Meanwhile, Clyde Konman pretending to be Troy Sooner was living in Hong Kong with his female accomplice, Miqua Savior. While she was visiting New York, it was a twist of fate that the two met at a social event. She was from Belize and Faith's older half-sister.

Miqua's mother and Faith's father were childhood sweethearts. When her mother became pregnant, he left Belize, came to the United States and promised to send for them, but he never did.

With no means of financial support from Miqua's father and always struggling to make ends meet, her mother would always state, "Your father deserted us and left us with nothing. He went to America and married a rich woman. Together, they had a daughter named Faith. She grew up having it all, and everything she has belongs to you as well."

Her ill and impoverished mother passed away two years ago. Consequently, Miqua came up with an elaborate scheme to avenge her father's betrayal. When she read about Faith's company and saw her on cable, Miqua along with Clyde came up with a diabolical plan to destroy Faith and her company. She pretended to be a real estate broker, as well as the owner of a private lending company, Real Estate Company, and a commercial building.

Clyde faked at being an attorney. He knew the real Troy Sooner, because they were lovers; he was able to get in and out of the townhouse and play the cruelest role of his life. Knowledgeable in real estate law, wills, and trusts, he could have tricked the most prestigious law firm into making him their senior partner. He even designed the web page for Troy. Since the site was not due to expire for another two years, he quickly replaced Troy's photo with his own. Before leaving the country, he reloaded Troy's image on the site. The plot worked.

Unfortunately, Faith never knew she had a half-sister, and Miqua never knew the real story, because when their father passed away, he also left Faith's mother with nothing.■

Serenity on Fire

After a night of invigorating sex with her fiancé, Serenity Jones woke up the next day exhausted. Despite her groggy state, she decided to do some last minute shopping for Christmas and Kwanzaa gifts, but an unexpected act and the mysterious events that were about to transpire, would leave her in a state of shock, anger, and disbelief.

Serenity was an illustrator who worked for some of the most prestigious companies. Born and raised in Chicago, she attended a well-known university in Evanston, Illinois and received her Bachelor's Degree in Fine Arts. For three years, she worked as a freelance sketch artist for major magazines, book publishers, and advertising agencies.

At age twenty-five, she left Chicago for New York City and moved into a one-bedroom apartment in SoHo, a trendy neighborhood known for its art galleries, high-end shops, restaurants, and nightclubs. Her rent was twenty-five hundred dollars a month, but she was not rich. Because she was an independent contractor, her income was sporadic. There were months when she made very little or no money at all.

Her parents, who still lived in Chicago, would help her financially, but when her father had an accident on his job and could no longer work, the extra cushion, which she had come to rely on, was limited.

Born in 1978, Serenity was a change of life baby. Her parents were in their late forties when they had her. She had an older brother who was sixteen when she came into the world. At age eighteen, he left home to enlist in the Marines. During furloughs, he would come into town but never spent much time with the family. Over the years, she had very little contact with him. The last she heard, he had retired from the service and was living in the Philippines with his wife and three children.

While growing up, she always sensed there was some bitterness on her brother's part, because her parents doted so much of their attention on her. There was talk that he and her parents never saw eye to eye on anything, and eventually, they had a falling out. She always felt it was because of her that he left so abruptly. But as she grew older, she understood that her brother was at that stage in life where it was all about him and his career, and families do have disputes, so it was not necessarily because of her that he became distant.

Two weeks before Christmas, Serenity attended a party given by the founder of a major advertising agency. The gala took place at a well-known restaurant in Upper Manhattan; over five hundred guests attended the affair. There was enough food to feed several nations and more liquor than all the bars in the city could muster up.

People were mingling and gossiping about the latest happenings in the business world. There was talk that the publisher of a men's health magazine was caught doing one of his junior executives in a seedy motel. The wife hired a private eye to follow her CEO husband, because she suspected he was having an affair but never imagined it was with a man.

Folks were also chatting about one of the guests, who slept her way up the corporate ladder, got pregnant and sued the father for child support, but a DNA test proved that he was not the baby's daddy. The fact that he was married never deterred her from going after him, and since she slept with so many men, it was doubtful if she would ever learn who sired her child.

Serenity knew most of the guests at the party but was not one to participate in hearsay. For one thing, these folks would talk and say cruel things about others behind their backs and then turn around and laugh and grin in their faces as though they were the best of friends.

Her grandmother would say, "The dog that brings the bone will carry the bone. If a person comes to you and talks or makes offensive comments about someone, that same individual will go back to others and make the same remarks about you." Therefore, throughout the night, Serenity made a point to avoid those blabbermouths.

The bash ended around three in the morning. Unbeknown to anyone, it was snowing, and three inches had already fallen. Most of the guests had their own means of transportation or lived nearby.

Serenity would have taken the bus, but she decided to take a cab. Taking the subway was out of the question. The last time she went underground, it was on a hot and humid day. Because of a mechanical malfunction, the train was stuck on the tracks for almost two hours. She started to hyperventilate and had a panic attack. Just from that incident alone, she vowed never to use the subway system.

The snow was coming down fast and furious. There were hardly any pedestrians on the streets or cars on the roads, but there were taxicabs galore.

For almost thirty minutes, Serenity was trying to hail one. Most were off-duty, and a few unoccupied cabs passed her by. As she started to walk toward the bus stop, she heard the sound of a honking horn. When she turned to check, it was a yellow cab, attempting to get her attention. The cabby slowed down and came to a complete stop. When the door opened, she got into the cab.

"Hello," said the driver.

"Good evening, West Broadway and Spring Street, please," she said.

The driver then said, "I was about to go off duty and turn in for the night. This is no time to be out all alone and stuck in a blizzard. Are you a tourist, or do you live here?"

"No, I live here, am originally from Chicago and moved here three years ago. I was coming from a Christmas party. Had I known snow was in the forecast, I would have stayed home. As much as I love the snow, getting stuck in it or being ill-prepared is no laughing matter, especially late at night."

"You mean early in the morning," laughed the driver.

Looking at her watch, she realized what he meant and chuckled; it was three-thirty in the morning.

From the moment Serenity stepped into the cab, the driver had the gift for gab. He introduced himself as Pierre Lamazé. He came to the United States five years ago from the island of Martinique, the birthplace of Joséphine, Napoleon's wife, a point he was so pompous to make.

Pierre was from the town of Le Lamentin, where his parents owned a sugarcane farm and a processing plant. He came to New York on a student visa to study computer programming and information technology and started to drive a taxicab to help pay for his college tuition. Since he had completed his studies, he would return home to take over and expand his family's business by having a presence on the World Wide Web.

By now, she was in awe of this man and talked about her line of work. As a self-employed illustrator, she met and worked with some of the most influential people in various industries but never liked working in one place too long or being part of that corporate culture. She was willing to forsake the security and benefits, which working for just one company would have provided, because she enjoyed being her own boss and working on her terms.

Arriving at her destination, she paid Pierre.

Before she got out of the cab, he asked, "Can we get together and have dinner one night? My hours are very flexible."

She responded, "That would be nice. My name is Serenity Jones, and here is my business card with my cell phone number. I am usually home after 6 PM. It was a pleasure meeting you, and thanks for stopping and picking me up."

In a crafty tone, he said, "It was my pleasure, Serenity. I am looking forward to seeing more of you before I leave New York."

When Serenity entered her apartment, it was after four in the morning. She was tired and at the same time excited. She removed her wet shoes and clothes and got into her nightgown. She was cold and decided to turn on the heat; it would take about thirty minutes for the place to get warm. During the winter months, she always kept the radiators off to save energy and money.

While lying in bed, she could not get Pierre off her mind, and the fact that he came from a wealthy family made him even more desirable. He was handsome, communicative, and downright tempting. After romanticizing about him, she finally fell asleep.

When Serenity woke up, it was 9:30 AM. She went into the kitchen to prepare breakfast. When she checked her voice mail, there was a message from Pierre.

"Hello, Serenity, it was such a joy meeting and talking with you this morning. I miss you already. Let us get together for dinner next week. You can call me with your answer at this number. Au revoir."

When she heard his voice, her body started to burn with desire. His voice alone had her dashing into the shower and positioning herself under the cool running water. Knowing then that he had captured her body, heart, and soul, she hurriedly returned his call and invited him over for dinner, next Friday evening at eight o'clock.

A major book publisher had called Serenity with a rush job. The company wanted her to design a cover and do several illustrations for a cookbook, which was going to print in two weeks. The artist hired to do the work came down with a grave illness while vacationing abroad and would not recuperate for several weeks.

Serenity had three days to complete the undertaking. Ordinarily, she would have declined the job, because she did not like clients calling her on such short notice, but the money the publisher was offering her was too good to turn down.

After working long hours, she completed the task; for her work, she received six thousand dollars. Because she did such a remarkable job, the publisher offered her a two-year non-exclusive contract. Since she would still be able to work for other companies, and the incentives and the money they were putting forward were beyond her expectations, she accepted their offer.

It was now Friday, and Serenity was up early preparing and cooking for tonight's dinner with Pierre.

She had some errands to run and left around two in the afternoon. When she returned home, it was almost 6 PM. She had two hours to get the place ready. She set the table and placed a bottle of wine in the chiller.

At exactly 7:45 PM, the doorbell rang. It was Pierre. He kissed her on the cheek and gave her a long yellow stem rose. She returned the kiss and thanked him for his kindness.

He said, "Each day, I was thinking about you. While driving, I had trouble concentrating and almost had an accident. Now that I am here, my heart is telling me that I have found my true love."

When she heard those words, her body went numb; she said, "When I got into your cab, I sensed a love connection between us."

He read her like a hardback and understood then that she was now under his reign.

She placed dinner in the oven, set the temperature on warm and stated, "Dinner will be ready in one hour."

She sat next to him on the sofa; they began to talk. Almost immediately, she was becoming hot and horny. They started to kiss and then slowly undressed each other. She led him into the bedroom and their naked and sweltering bodies became one.

Pierre was such a tremendous force that he took their lovemaking to an amazing greatness. They were like two parallel dancers aiming to outmaneuver each other. As soon as the lovemaking ended, she was ready to leave everything behind and spend the rest of her life with him.

When she woke up, Pierre was gone, but he left a note on her pillow:

Dear Serenity:
Last night was unforgettable. Will talk to you soon.
Pierre

Serenity and Pierre never ate dinner. She completely forgot about the stuffed chicken, brown rice, and vegetables left in the warm oven all night. The chicken was so dry that a famished lion would have thought twice before devouring the fowl; the bacterium content alone was enough to kill several cats. She ended up tossing the food, which she had spent so much time and effort preparing, but it did not matter. The sexual pleasure she got from Pierre was more fulfilling than any cuisine she could have ever created.

On December 22, Pierre called Serenity early in the morning with good news.

"I am leaving for Martinique on December 26 and will return in four weeks. My parents called and asked me to come home and take care of the business while they visit relatives and friends abroad. I would like to see you before I leave."

In heated ecstasy, she asked, "Can you come over this evening?"

He answered, "I'll be there around eight."

Pierre arrived at Serenity's place. She was so delighted to see him that her body was an inferno. They kissed, quickly undressed and started to make tempestuous love.

While the lovemaking was in full speed, he moaned and screamed, "Serenity, will you marry me?"

Without any uncertainty, her answer was "Yes!"

He then said, "When I get back from my trip, I will tie-up loose ends and quit my job at the cab company. On May 1, we will leave for Martinique and plan the most elaborate and memorable wedding."

The lovemaking continued with Serenity being over the moon with passion.

He said, "I will miss you."

She said, "When you land in Martinique, call me."

Eventually, the lovemaking ended on a high note. In an idyllic state, she closed her eyes and went to sleep.

When Serenity woke up the next day, it was late afternoon.

Pierre was gone, but he left another note on her pillow:

Dear Serenity:
Sweet dreams, my pretty one!
Love always,
Pierre

The contract that Serenity signed with the book publisher was extremely accommodating. Since she was planning to move to Martinique with Pierre, she would be able to e-mail her illustrations to their art department. If she had to fly to New York for special meetings, the company would pay for her airfare, lodging, and meals.

She had it all worked out. Since her lease would expire in July, she would ask management if they would release her from the last three months. Her lease did not allow subletting, but finding a renter to take over her apartment was not going to be a problem. People were willing to give up their first-born or sell their soul to the devil to live in SoHo, especially in her building, where quite a few celebrities resided.

She then contacted her parents and told them the wonderful news. She would fly them to Martinique for the big event, but because her father was not able to travel, it would be just her mother attending. When Serenity told her parents about Pierre, they were extremely happy for her.

While in college, she fell in love with a student who was studying international politics and economics, but he won a Rhodes Scholarship to Oxford University in England. They kept in touch, but ultimately, his letters and e-mails stopped. While at Oxford, he met a fellow student, fell in love and married her.

The last Serenity heard he was living in California with his wife and two children.

She often thought about him and wondered what her life would have been like had she followed him to England. Although she dated often, he was her first love.

When her career took off, meeting someone and getting married were distant thoughts, until she met Pierre.

Her mother would always say, "When you are not looking, you will find someone."

As luck would have it, that someone was Pierre.

For the next couple of weeks, Serenity was online looking for legal requirements to get married in Martinique and searching for romantic spots to hold the nuptial and wedding reception.

An original birth certificate or a copy with the raised seal was required. Since Pierre was already a citizen, and they would be living in Martinique permanently, she did not need a residency card. Three months prior to the marriage, a medical certificate and proof of a blood test were mandatory. Other needed documents were a certificate of good conduct and verification of single status.

While browsing for a venue to have the ceremony and reception, she came across a villa for rent with the option to buy; it would be the perfect spot to hold their big affair.

The 5,000 square feet country-style house sat on two acres of land and came with four bedrooms, four-baths, a rebuilt kitchen, a swimming pool, and a gazebo. The dining room and living room with their spectacular views of the countryside and ocean were spacious enough to accommodate at least three hundred guests.

The rent was fifteen hundred dollars a month, less than what she was paying for her one bedroom apartment in SoHo. She would discuss with Pierre about renting or buying the house and having the affair there.

It was mid-January, and Serenity had not heard from Pierre. Being so busy with work and shopping online for a wedding gown and bridal accessories, she could not believe how fast the time went.

Management wanted to know when she was planning to vacate the apartment. A long list of people were lining up like ducks in a row to rent her place. Some individuals were even willing to pay a year's rent in advance, sight unseen. She would leave at the end of April.

In the meantime, she was starting to worry about Pierre; she thought something had happened to him. When she tried to reach him on his cell phone, there was no signal. She neglected to get the phone number of the taxi service where he worked and had no idea where he lived.

It was now the end of January, and Serenity still had not heard from Pierre.

She was running low on cash and usually kept one thousand dollars in a cookie jar for emergencies. She decided to go to the bank to withdraw some money from her savings account. Her last bank statement showed a balance of ninety thousand dollars. In her checking account, she kept enough money to pay her rent and bills and for miscellaneous expenses.

When she got to the bank and handed the teller the withdrawal slip for fifteen hundred dollars, the clerk said, "That account is closed."

With a startled look on her face, Serenity responded, "That's impossible. There must be some mistake. I never closed that account. Please check again."

The clerk patiently rechecked and said, "According to our records, you closed that account on December 23."

"No, I did not," said Serenity in an angry and a defensive tone.

Finally, she asked to speak to the manager. What she was about to hear would leave her speechless.

The bank manager explained, "On December 23, you came into the bank and wanted to close your savings account, because you were planning to move to Martinique."

"But I never came into the bank that day," she insisted.

"Well, unless you have an identical twin sister, it was you who came into this bank and closed your savings account; you also withdrew six thousand dollars from your checking account, and your balance is now ten dollars. If you do not believe me, I have proof."

The manager then went on his computer and uploaded the security tape, which showed her and a man coming into the bank that day at approximately 9:30 AM. After seeing that tape, she recognized the man; it was Pierre.

Yet, she still could not recall coming into the bank with him and said, "That woman on the tape is a dead ringer, but that is not me. I would certainly remember if I came into the bank that day. That imposter stole my money. What action is your bank going to take to rectify this terrible error and have that woman arrested?"

However, the biggest shock came when the manager uploaded a photocopied form that she completed to close the account, along with her photo, signature, and thumbprint. They were all a match.

The manager then said, "If you suspect you were a victim of fraud, you must contact law enforcement immediately and file a complaint. The bank will not take any further measures until we hear from the proper authorities."

Reluctantly, she thanked the bank manager, because she knew it was fruitless to pursue the matter. Where would she begin? Embarrassed by the whole incident, she left in an unsettling mood.

When she got home, there was an envelope slipped under her door: *The enclosed check for January's rent came back stamped insufficient funds. Please remit future payments in the form of a money order. If we do not receive payment in ten days, management will tack on a late fee.*

Now broke and at the brink of being evicted, Serenity started to ask herself, *How did I allow myself to be taken in by such a trickster.* She thought about what the bank manager said, but she knew it was a waste of time to go to the police. She knew nothing about this man and had no idea where he lived or worked. When she got into his cab, she never noticed if his driver's license, photo, and taximeter were in separate frames, which all three had to be visible to passengers.

She contacted the Taxi and Limousine Commission and explained that she was looking for a driver named Pierre Lamazé. She gave them the date, time, pick-up, and drop-off points and mentioned there was a blizzard that morning, but there was no record on file of a driver with that name. Since she did not have the hack number or a receipt, the agency could not assist her. She only knew the car was yellow and assumed it was a legitimate taxicab.

Racking her brain about December 23 became Serenity's fixation. The memory of that day was slowly coming back. She remembered getting a call from Pierre on December 22. He was coming to see her that evening before he left for his trip. They went to bed and made love for several hours.

When she woke up the next day, it was almost three in the afternoon. She was feeling lethargic but attributed the mood to her dynamic sex with him. She recalled reading the note that he left on her pillow and then went shopping. From that point on, she had no recollection of going to the bank, withdrawing money or giving ninety-six thousand dollars to anyone, much less to Pierre.

She speculated that he must have drugged or hypnotized her, took her to the bank and manipulated her to withdraw the money from her savings account. Since her mother was the joint holder of the checking account, and both of their signatures were required, he could not sway her to close that account but was clever enough to have her remove most of the money. He brought her back to the apartment, tucked her into bed and left. What other explanation was there that would cause her to block out the strange occurrences that occurred that day.

She finally got it. The man she fell madly in love with was a diabolical con artist. He pegged her right from the start, and she became his innocent victim. She started to question, *How could I have fallen into such a vile trap? Most likely, he never attended college, was probably using a fake name and was not from Martinique. In all likelihood, his vehicle was a replica of an official yellow cab.*

She sat in her apartment and wept for hours but finally pulled herself together and called her parents. She told them the complete sordid details and asked if she could borrow some money to help carry her over for the next several months. Her parents agreed and wired enough money into her checking account to pay for four months' rent. It was too late for her to change her mind about moving. Management had already found a couple. They signed a two-year lease and would move into her place on June 1.

Serenity was busy looking for a place to live, but at her current financial state, the rents were more than she could afford. She went back to Chicago and moved in with her parents. She thought about the mess she made of her life after meeting Pierre but believed his day would come sooner than later and reaffirmed, *A person like you can never use people, bilk them out of their money and think you will never get caught. So, you had better watch out Pierre, because God don't like ugly, and He's not too keen on beauty.*

After Pierre broke her heart and pilfered her money, it took three years for Serenity to get her personal life and finances back on track. From that disastrous affair, she learned to conduct a thorough background check on a potential mate before giving her heart to any man.

She would hear and read about people who became victims of deceit. Blinded by love, they lost all of their life's savings. Even though many of these individuals saw the warning signs that things were not quite right, they still became targets of ruthless swindlers. Yet, she was determined not to make the same mistakes again. Now thirty-two and wiser, she was ready to meet that special someone. Those past come-on lines would never catch her off guard.

Serenity was now living in a duplex apartment, which was not too far from her parents' home. She was so busy that turning down jobs became common. Well known in the business and social circles, she had no problems meeting men. Although she dated decent and hardworking gents, not one was able to find or chime her G-spot.

She did join a place of worship, which had over three thousand members, but for every ten females, there was one male. The competition for finding a man was extremely stiff. Many of the male members were married or in committed relationships, and the long-standing female members had already latched on to the remaining eligible bachelors. She had a much better chance at meeting an alien from planet Neptune.

Since the pickings were so slim, she decided to check a matchmaking service, whose brochure she received in the mail. The name of the agency was, *The Best Little Matchmaker in Town*, which had an office downtown on Michigan Avenue.

She went online to see if the company had a presence on the World Wide Web, but it did not. To be on the safe side, she contacted the Better Business Bureau to see if there were any complaints filed against the service. According to their records, there were no grievances on file. She then called the matchmaker's number and made an appointment to meet with a representative the following day.

When Serenity woke up the next morning, it was a bright and windy day. She felt blessed and believed her significant other was just around the corner. She skipped breakfast and went straight to the matchmaker's headquarters. The receptionist led her into a luxurious office, which had floor to ceiling windows with panoramic views of the Chicago River and skyline.

A distinguished looking woman introduced herself as Veronica Lae, the co-founder and CEO of the company. The two shook hands and sat down.

Ms. Lae asked, "How did you hear about our service?"

"I received your brochure in the mail," answered Serenity.

"How nice," said Veronica, who then went on to discuss how the business got started.

"My partner and I began this matchmaking business ten years ago. We did not make any money during the first three years but now have offices throughout the world and moved into this building two years ago. We have over one million members. Since our inception, five thousand couples have gotten married, and eighty percent of them are still together. Before anyone can join our service, we do a thorough background check. If we discover that an individual has not been truthful about his or her employment or financial standing or single status, we will deny membership and refund their money minus administrative costs. You will receive a questionnaire; based on your answers, we will match you with men who share your specific values and requirements and send you their profiles and vice versa. You will receive a minimum of ten matches a month. The annual membership fee is five thousand dollars."

Serenity then asked, "Why isn't your service on the World Wide Web?"

With a convincing smile, Veronica responded, "Our members prefer finding a companion using a more traditional service, such as ours. For many singles, the human contact is preferred over the air of mystery when meeting someone online."

After listening to Veronica and the fact that the service did a detailed check on its members, Serenity felt confident enough to join. She received reading materials, which outlined the role and objectives of the service, a questionnaire, an application, and a two-page contract.

The receptionist took her into a private office. There, Serenity completed all the papers, carefully read the agreement, added her signature and paid the membership fee with a check. The receptionist came in, took her picture and scanned important documents into the computer, and along with her personal and financial information, Serenity's profile was now on file.

Veronica came in and asked, "Do you have any additional questions?"

"No," replied Serenity.

"Well, it was a pleasure meeting you, and thank you for joining our service. If you have any questions or need further assistance, please do not hesitate to contact us. We are here to serve you and meet your romantic needs. You will be hearing from us shortly," said Veronica. Serenity thanked her and the receptionist for their help and left feeling jubilant.

Two weeks later, Serenity's dreams were about to come true. As she was getting ready to turn in for the night, her phone rang. When she picked up the receiver, the voice on the other end said, "Hello, may I speak to Serenity Jones?"

"Speaking," answered Serenity.

"This is Jack Cisco. I received your profile from The Best Little Matchmaker in Town."

"Oh yes," she said. "I just became a member. Do you live in Chicago?"

"No, I live in Portugal for the time being. I am an art dealer, travel ninety-percent of the time and plan to visit your country next week; perhaps we could get together for a meeting and dinner."

She could not reply fast enough and said, "That would be wonderful. You can usually reach me after 8 PM."

"I will definitely contact you with my travel plans in a couple of days and look forward to seeing you," said Jack.

"Likewise, and thank you for calling," she said in an upbeat tone.

His voice was so sexy that she broke out in a cold sweat. After getting off the phone, Serenity was perspiring and having hot flashes as if she were going through the change of life. She removed her clothing, went to bed and slept in the buff, something she had not done for a while.

The next day, Serenity called Veronica to inform her that an interested member had called. When she mentioned Jack Cisco's name, Veronica said, "I am thrilled he contacted you. After you passed the background check, I faxed your profile to Mr. Cisco a week ago. In my opinion, you two are a perfect match. I will send you his profile by courier today."

In one hour, a messenger delivered the packet. When she opened the package and saw his photo, he looked vaguely familiar. She could not put her hands on it but kept thinking she had seen this man before. Suddenly, it came to her. He resembled one of the deacons at her church.

Jack was extremely handsome, and his bio was incredible. He dealt in rare art pieces, had homes in several countries and was the owner of an art gallery in Spain. He was forty-two years old, never married and had no children. His annual income was over five million dollars.

Serenity thought she had finally hit pay dirt and found her true partner for life.

On Sunday, Jack called Serenity. Since he was planning to fly to Wyoming on business, he would make a stopover in Chicago and would be arriving at O'Hare International Airport on Wednesday at 2 PM. So overjoyed, she was counting the hours when he would walk into her life. *I can feel it in my heart that Jack is the one*, she thought.

It was Wednesday morning, and Serenity woke up on top of the world. She was going to meet Jack for dinner at his hotel, but she could not decide on what to wear. She did not want to dress too sexy. Yet, she did not want to come over as a prude and selected a navy blue satin dress and red pumps. To highlight her face, she would wear black pearl earrings.

When Serenity arrived at the hotel, she went straight to Jack's room and knocked on the door. When the door opened, she was ready to be his lover. In person, he was drop-dead gorgeous. He was tall and alluring, had a clean-cut beard and was downright luscious. The two hugged and were delighted to meet.

She asked, "How was your flight?"

He replied, "The trip was long, but I kept thinking about you, and before I knew it, the plane was landing. When I first saw your photo, I sensed there was something between us. As I read your profile, my feelings for you grew stronger. Now that I am here, we are destined to be together." After hearing those expressions, she was ready to leap into bed with him.

Because this was Jack's first time in Chicago, he made reservations for dinner at a restaurant in the hotel. He and Serenity ordered drinks, talked about their future together and gazed at each other like lovesick adolescents. After dinner, they decided to go back to his room. His deep sexy voice had her yearning for him. If he had asked her to, she would have run off with him without having any misgivings.

Soft music was piping into his suite.

He asked, "May I have this dance with you?"

"Yes," she said.

Suddenly, she began to do slow bumps and grinds and pressed her body next to his. She was getting hotter and wetter by the minute. He sensed she was ready for him. Like a potent lion, he removed her clothing. She surrendered to him like a disciplined lioness. They landed in bed and made love as though 2012 was seconds away.

She shouted, "Do me baby! Do me now! Don't stop, you naughty tiger!" Being in complete control, he gave her the most erotic jolt of her being. To her, he was an aficionado when it came to detecting and tantalizing her sensual spots.

The lovemaking went on until he could no longer continue his exhilarating activities with her. He finally fell asleep, but she was still making an effort to hold on to those electrifying sensations.

When Serenity woke up, she knew Jack was going to be the man in her life. She took a shower and dressed. Jack was still asleep. She kissed him on his forehead.

As she went to sit on the sofa, she noticed a silver attaché case on the table. She was not a nosy person, but she could not refrain from looking into that briefcase.

When she opened the case, there were numerous credit cards, five thousand dollars in cash, and an envelope marked, *Confidential*. In the envelope were three passports, each belonging to Jack Cisco, Veronica Lae, and of all people, Pierre Lamazé? All three were nationals of

Martinique. With tears in her eyes and anger in her heart, she quickly ran out of the room leaving the suitcase and Jack Cisco behind.

When Serenity got home, she was stunned. The fact that Veronica knew Pierre was just too much of a coincidence. She understood the relationship between Veronica and Jack, because he was a member of her matchmaking service. Yet, she could not comprehend Pierre's role in this triangle and decided to play amateur detective.

She called Veronica's office, but there was a busy signal. She decided to leave home, confront Veronica in person and inquire about Pierre, but when she got to the office, there was a security lock on the doorknob.

She checked with the building manager who said, "The owners of The Best Little Matchmaker in Town disappeared, owing three months' rent. They also duped unsuspecting people looking for mates out of their money. I hope you are not one of those victims, because if you are, you will have to stand in line. There have been thousands of complaints filed against these people, but law enforcement will probably never catch them. These rogues are insightful and almost never get caught."

Serenity stood there as though someone had stuck a knife in her back. Since she knew where one of the crooks was, she would immediately contact law enforcement.

When Serenity got back to her apartment, she checked her voice mail: "Hi, Serenity, this is Jack. An emergency has come up, and I have to leave the country. I am in the air now and will contact you when I reach my destination. By the way, you were awesome last night. Farewell, my love!" After hearing that message, she screamed so loud that her chandelier started to vibrate. It was too late to call the police.

A month later, Serenity got her credit card bill. A cash advance for five thousand dollars appeared on her statement. Just when it seemed things could not have gotten any worse, she received her bank statement showing an overdraft of five thousand dollars. She knew then that three despicable characters took her for a devious ride on trickery road.

Trying to figure out how this could have happened again, she took out a copy of her membership application.

The information she provided on that form gave the three crooks every opportunity to fleece her. By providing the matchmaking service with her social security number, credit card number, and bank account information, she frankly said, "My money is your money."

Sitting in her apartment, Serenity thought about the blunders she made while searching for love. It was as though she neglected to exercise common sense when she met Pierre and Jack. Often, she would hear the elders say, "Nowadays, common sense is not that common."

She placed a freeze on her credit card and disputed the bill. Eventually, the creditor removed the charge and gave her a new account number, but the bank overdraft was never resolved.

Two years later, Serenity's money situation was sound again. She was busy as usual with her illustrations, had amassed a large clientele base and hired an assistant to oversee the administrative components of the business. At the end of the year, her company made a profit of two hundred and fifty thousand dollars.

While Serenity was surfing the Internet, breaking news scrolled across her screen: *Three People Arrested and Charged with Fraud.*

While reading the article, she hollered, "Halleluiah, there is a God!"

The Martinique authorities had arrested Veronica Lae, Jack Cisco, and Pierre Lamazé and charged them with racketeering, credit card fraud, and identity theft, and more charges were imminent.

According to the piece, The Best Little Matchmaker in Town bilked members out of millions of dollars. Singles from around the world thought they were meeting that ideal person, but most of the matches given to them were fictitious.

While conducting their stings, the three villains owed back rents in the seven figures. Whenever authorities were about to move in on them, the trio would disappear, but they slipped up in Martinique. Veronica, Pierre, and Jack were cousins.

After reading that exposé, all the pieces finally fell into place. Pierre and Jack were stingers in a honeycomb, and

Veronica, the queen bee, was the brains behind the whole setup.

How these people were able to draw her into their web of deceit confused Serenity. Because her phone number and address were unlisted, she questioned, *How did they get my address to mail me their brochure?* Then, she remembered telling Pierre that she was originally from Chicago. Since he mentioned he had studied computer programming and information technology, she figured that he must have been tracking her every move on the Internet.

Pierre probably guessed that I was still stuck on stupid, but as I predicted, he got caught. And now all three of those rascals will definitely suffer the reprimands for their cunning acts, she concluded with a big smile.

Despite all the mayhem and stupidity that plagued her life, Serenity was still lonely and longing for a man. At least for now, she decided that being alone was a much better choice than being with someone who would make her life a living nightmare. ∎

About The Author

Vivienne Diane Neal was born in 1946 and started to write fictional short stories in 2007. She is a storyteller with a wicked sense of humor. Her story ideas come from daily observations of people, places, and objects and from actual TV civil court cases.

Her first book, Making Dollar$ And Cent$ Out Of Online Dating, is a true-life and humorous account as to why and how she got into the dating business and the problems she has encountered in the past while trying to keep afloat in the ever-changing world of the Internet dating business.

In 2009, she authored and self-published her second book, Shades of Deception, a collection of ten fictional short stories centering on diverse men and women, who in their speedy search for love, romance, and bliss, become the targets and victims of deceit, betrayal, fraud, revenge, and scandal.

Now semi-retired, Vivienne write articles on dating, love, romance, relationships, and other topics of interests.

Sites to Visit:

http://oneworldsinglesblog.net

http://lulu.com/spotlight/hmcs1946

http://www.smashwords.com/profile/view/hmcs

http://www.amazon.com/-/e/B003ONO6G4

http://www.amazon.co.uk/-/e/B003ONO6G4

www.ingramcontent.com/pod-product-compliance
Lightning Source LLC
Chambersburg PA
CBHW052136170626
46812CB00004B/1455